This Is Paradise

STORIES

KRISTIANA KAHAKAUWILA

HOGARTH

London   New York

Published in the United States by Hogarth, an imprint of the Crown Publishing Group, a division of Random House, Inc., New York.
www.crownpublishing.com

HOGARTH is a trademark of the Random House Group Limited, and the H colophon is a trademark of Random House, Inc.

Library of Congress Cataloging-in-Publication Data
Kahakauwila, Kristiana.
This is paradise : stories / Kristiana Kahakauwila. — First edition.
pages   cm
1. Hawaii—Social life and customs—21st century—Fiction.
I. Title.
PS3611.A3455T48 2013
813'.6—dc23
2012040063

ISBN 978-0-7704-3625-4
eISBN 978-0-7704-3626-1

Printed in the United States of America

Book design by Lauren Dong
Jacket design by Christopher Brand
Jacket photograph: David W. Dellinger

10 9 8 7 6 5 4 3 2 1

First Edition

For my parents,
Nancy and David,
'o wau nō me ka ho'omaika'i

CONTENTS

THIS IS PARADISE

Midmorning the lifeguards fan across the beach and push signposts into the sand. The same picture is on all of them: a stick figure, its arms aloft, its circle head drowning in a set of triangle waves. CAUTION, the signs read. DANGEROUS UNDERTOW.

We ignore it. We've gone out at Mākaha and Makapu'u before. We've felt Yokes pull us under. We are not afraid of the beaches and breaks here in Waikīkī. We are careless, in fact, brazen. So when we see her studying the warning, chewing the right side of her lip, we laugh. *Jus' like da kine, scared of da water. Haoles, yeah.*

The tourist girl is white. They're all white to us unless they're black. She has light brown hair, a pointed nose, eyebrows neatly plucked into a firm line. She wears a white bikini with red polka dots. Triangle-cut top, ruffled bottom. We shake our heads at her. Our 'ehu hair, pulled into ponytails, bounces against our necks. Our bikinis are carefully cut pieces with cross-back straps and lean bottoms. We surf in these, sista. We don't have time for ruffles and ruching. But she does, like every other tourist. Her blue-and-white-striped hotel towel labels her for what she is.

So why do we look at her as we pass? Why do we notice her out of the hundreds of others? Do we already know she's marked, special in some way?

At the high tide line Cora Jones and Kaila Ka'awa pull on rashguards to protect against the trade winds, which are wailing this morning. The rest of us pretend we don't have chicken skin. We strap our leashes to our ankles, careful to piece the Velcro together, and then we jump on our boards and feel them skim across the surface of the water. Arching our backs, our hips pressed into hard fiberglass, we dig the water with our hands. We raise one foot for balance, and because we know we are silhouetted against the horizon, we hold our heads high, we point our toes. Our bodies curve upward, like smiles, beckoning those on shore to follow.

When we look back, the tourist girl is approaching the ocean's edge. She walks into the water, the small waves lapping at her feet, ankles, knees, chest. We see her dip her shoulders into the whitewash. We don't tell her to stay away from the retaining wall in front of Baby Queens or that today the current is moving from 'Ewa to Diamond Head. We paddle, and in a moment, we've left her behind.

Only local folks leave us money, placing it on top of the television in an envelope with the word "Housekeeping" printed across the front. We split the cash, tucking it into our shoes where management won't look for it.

We, the women of Housekeeping, get left other things, too, but by accident. The Japanese leave behind useful items: tubes of sunscreen, beach floaties, snorkel gear, unopened boxes of cereal, half-filled bottles of American whiskey, brand-new packets of travel tissues decorated with Choco-Cat and Hello Kitty, which our youngest girls love. The tissues we take. Even when management checks the pockets of our uniforms, they never think to confiscate packets of tissues. We don't get in trouble for bringing those home. The rest we throw into trash bags or hide on the bottom shelf of our carts to leave at the loading dock for night security. Management doesn't check their pockets.

What mainland Americans leave behind makes us blush: used condoms under the bed, a turquoise bra with thick cups like soup bowls, pornographic magazines. We find a single blue sandal, a hairbrush tangled with yellow hair, a vibrating toothbrush, a stuffed bear with a missing arm and glass eyes. Such intimate pieces to forget.

Today we have been cleaning rooms for five hours, since six in the morning. Tucking the bottom sheets at least eight times, disinfecting the sinks and bathtubs, vacuuming the dark brown carpets. We have cleaned twelve rooms and have eight more to go. We pause in the hallway. We don't have time to rest, but we do anyway, just for a moment. The door to room 254 is open, and we watch a young woman tie a white wrap around her waist. Her polka-dot bathing suit is damp and turns the white fabric sheer, the red dots shining through like mosquito bites. She catches us watching her. "You don't need to replace the towels," she says, smiling. "Conserve water." Her teeth are coins, flat and shiny. We want to tell her to wear a thicker skirt, but it's not our place to speak to guests.

A young man appears from behind the wall and walks around the foot of the bed: "I already left mine on the floor."

The girl rolls her eyes. "Then pick it up," she scolds. She turns to give us an exasperated smile, and we are reminded of our eldest daughters: impatient with non-sense, bossing their brothers, keeping the house. This girl, like our girls, is the type a mother can depend on to *do* things: drive Grandmother to a doctor's appointment, cook breakfast for Papa, dress and feed the babies before school. We smile back at her. We feel as if we can trust her.

The young man finally emerges from the bedroom— shoelaces untied, hat pulled low over his eyes—and she smacks him lightly on the arm. "You take longer than a girl," she says. She laughs, a light, tinkling giggle. He laughs. They look at us, so we laugh. At the end of the hall, she turns and waves at us. We nod, small smiles tightening our lips, and then we enter the room to make the beds.

We think of her for the rest of our shift, chuckling at her bossiness and cheer. When we return our carts, the manager doesn't bother to check our pockets, which makes this a good day, and we decide the American girl has brought us luck.

The hotel is strict about a great number of our activities. They have rules on how to store the carts, what time to punch in, what time to punch out, how to answer the phone (always start with "Aloha"), how to arrange the pillows on the bed, how to report suspicious activity. The last rule was created to fight terrorism, though we wonder what kind of terrorists would stay in Waikīkī. In fact, we don't entirely understand this rule or trust it. It seems designed only to make trouble for us. We've heard stories, after all, stories about workers like us who tried to obey the rule. Stories like the one about Janora Cabrera, who saw a man pressing a woman against a wall and reaching up her skirt on the penthouse floor. Janora told her shift manager about what she had seen. The shift manager reported it to the night auditor, who deferred to the daytime manager. Together, they reprimanded Janora. "You are only to report suspicious behavior," they told her. "You are not to involve yourself with our guests' lives."

Our shift ends at two in the afternoon, and we exit the hotel from the basement, a hot tunnel that smells of dryer sheets. This is where the housekeeping office is located and where we are kept, tucked away from the visitors who wander in and out of the front lobby. From here we cannot hear their sandals clap against the polished marble floors nor see their eyes widen as they first glimpse the Pacific through the glass windows of the lanai. We exit onto a sidewalk spotted with old gum stains and the faint red splatter of a spilled shave ice.

At the bus stop, waiting to go home, we laugh with one another. We talk of our husbands and our children. How fast they grow, our little ones, how quickly they move through school, through friends, through clothes. Already the youngest speak more English than we do, and the eldest make plans to go to college. We're proud of them, scared for them. We want them to go. We want them to stay in the house to help us. We even want, in some small part of our hearts, to send them back home to Pohnpei or Yap or Kosrae so they can really learn what it means to be one of us. Already they are American.

On the ride home, our shoulders ache and our shoes feel tight around our swollen feet. We close our eyes and let the bus's air-conditioning wash over us like a wave.

⌁

We tap the gas pedal, then hit the brakes again. Our cars lurch to a stop. Our heels and briefcases slide across the passenger seat, and one shoe drops to the floor with a hollow thunk. As successful career women we left work feel-

ing powerful, but the traffic at Kapi'olani and Kalākaua
has ended that. We might be the ones chosen to mold our
islands' future, but we're stuck like everyone else, our
cars moving at the speed of poi.

We stare into the four-story convention center, its
glass walls lending the impression of a squared fishbowl. A
dental convention is in town, and we watch as a cluster of
attendees crowd the escalator. On the ground floor they
shake hands and exchange business cards. One of them
reaches into his plastic goody-bag to show off a collection
of maps, pamphlets, and lastly some travel toothbrushes,
which causes riotous laughter among the group. We are
not privy to the joke, but our mouths are sticky from
nine hours at the office. We could use those toothbrushes
right now.

We could also use massages and an end to this traffic.
Esther Lu could use a glass of wine, which she would sip
on the couch when she finally reaches her condo. Laura
Tavares would like two hours of television, preferably
the Food Channel. The rest of us want a personal chef.
Lacking one, we'll probably call our parents and see what
they're having for dinner, which we do on more evenings
than we'd care to admit. One more benefit of returning
home to the islands.

Despite our tendency toward culinary laziness, our
exhaustion is not allowed to overtake us this evening.
Tonight, we're celebrating. Laura just submitted her proposal for a LEED-certified resort on Maui, and we hear

her firm will win the bid; Kiana Naone was promoted to Politics Editor at the *Honolulu Advertiser*; and Esther will take the lead on a high-profile murder case that all but promises her making partner in a year. After years of part-time jobs and student loans and late nights with a desk lamp's yellow light on our books, we've made it. Or are making it. Or are close to saying we will make it.

It doesn't hurt that we're from here. We are considered by our peers to be local women who've done well, left but come back, dedicated their education and mainland skills to putting this island right. We speak at civic club gatherings and native rights events. We are becoming pillars of the island community. We are growing into who we've always dreamt of being. But sometimes, late at night and alone beneath the hand-stitched Hawaiian quilts we can finally afford to purchase, we wish we had followed our law and grad school boyfriends to D.C. or Chicago. We could have foregone being pillars. We could have been regular women.

Meeting room doors are flung open and dentists stream from the fishbowl. The day's activities at the convention center are ended. The dentists cross the Ala Wai Canal, swarm the bridge on Kalākaua Avenue, and the traffic stands completely still as our cars are consumed by a mass of people armed with travel toothbrushes. Some jackass honks his horn like it's going to move the herd. The dentists all look so similar, with their neatly cut hair, ruler-straight teeth, and habit of striding with purpose, as if their assistance is urgently needed elsewhere. We can't help but wonder which of them are single.

In this moment of exit, their spirits high from presentations on the latest anesthetic or whitening solution, the dentists forget where they are. Hawai'i has less tropical flavor than they recall from the morning, less exoticism, less beauty. Waikīkī has become like any other city strip. We'd like to tell them that Waikīkī is nothing more than a succession of Hyatts and Courtyard by Marriotts, Cheesecake Factories and Planet Hollywoods, Señor Frogs and dingy Irish pubs with names like Murphy's and Callahan's. We'd like to tell them the real Hawai'i is elsewhere, hidden in the karaoke bars on King Street and on Waimānalo's ranch lands, in the view of the Mokes from Pillboxes and along the beach by Dillingham Air Strip, the portion of North Shore where only locals camp. We could tell them, but we say nothing.

Our cars inch forward. We stare out the windows, bored. A woman in a polka-dot bikini and pareo is shopping in one of the ABC convenience stores. Why do women from the Continent think they should shop in their bikinis? She buys two bags of Kona coffee, four boxes of chocolate-covered macadamia nuts, a string of cheap Pacific pearls, and a stack of postcards featuring various beaches all bathed in the reddish light of the same sunset. Her brother—same ski-jump nose, same narrowly set eyes—holds up a T-shirt, pointing proudly to the central image: a hula girl wearing a coconut bra, grass skirt, and lei. The hula girl's skin is fair, haole skin, and we're not sure if this makes the image better or worse.

The light changes. Our cars inch forward again. We return our gaze to the dentists, whose spouses are waiting for them in front of numerous hotel lobbies. The spouses are tired and hungry and pink as boiled shrimp from their day at the beach. The kids—all ages—are bored or playing video games or asking when they can next swim in the hotel pool. We pretend that, if on vacation ourselves, we would act differently—hike Koko Head, attend a bon dance, visit the Palace and learn about the Hawaiian monarchy—but deep down, we know we'd do the same as they: venture no farther than the nearest Starbucks.

In front of Denny's, one of the kids whines, "I wanted Mickey-ear pancakes," and the mother says to her husband, "Next year, Florida." We want to tell the boy we understand: Hawai'i lacks a Toon Town and roller coasters. And outside of Waikīkī, the native dress seems suspiciously similar to what's on sale at Macy's. Hawai'i is no fantasyland.

⌐~~⌐

Men fill the Lava Lounge the way sand fills a tidepool: at the edge of the rock walls and then creeping toward the center. A game is on—at the Lava Lounge, a game is always on—and a spontaneous moan issues from the bar. The men's faces tilt upward, in the direction of the big-screen TVs mounted above the top-shelf liquor, and their arms are crossed in such a way that their beer rests in the crooks of their left elbows. They speak to each other out of the corners of their mouths, analyzing plays and players and, maybe once, a woman who crosses their field of vision. They are not immune to us, but they aren't ready to pursue us yet either. In the meantime, we order dinner and describe the waves we caught this morning.

The women in the bar—the ones other than us local girls—are tourists or college students eager to start the night. They pretend to watch the game, but their Lycra skirts and jean short-shorts give them away. One girl— petite, barely twenty-one, if that—has tucked her sheer tank top into a neon orange skirt. When she bends over, we glimpse the top of a pink thong. She seems to enjoy bending over.

We want to tell her to wait, bide her time. Let the men drink and enjoy their game, and when they're good and ready, they'll notice you. But we know she won't listen to us. She's in a hurry to pair off, stake a claim, fall ecstatically into someone's arms or bed. Watching her, we feel we are being flung through time and space, that the rush of air on our faces is the world spinning faster for this girl, for all girls.

Our burgers arrive and we look at each other, surprised. Haven't we already hurled ourselves past this moment? Hasn't the fourth quarter ended? Haven't the men climbed down from their stools and taken up residence with a table of women? Isn't the night already careening to its end? A reggae band has assembled its drum set on the low wooden stage. The singer presses his mouth against the microphone: "One-two-three, check. One-two-three, check."

Our plates are cleared, the girl in the orange skirt rests her fingertips on the muscled arm of an army man, and we complain, as usual, about all these haoles coming on our land, even though we've come to Waikīkī. But where else can we go for a strip of bars and clubs? For our friends' band, and the other young locals we'll see? Why do we have to share it with all these tourists, military, college kids? We are just getting good and worked up when we spot the polka-dot girl from this morning. She stands at the entrance, hesitating, the spotlights outside illuminating her body, the soft curve of her hips, her small breasts. She's wearing a maroon dress, nothing flashy, simple in its loose cut, with a hemline that grazes her thighs. She glances furtively around the bar, then makes a beeline for an empty two-top, a high bar table with a pair of backless stools. A boy falls in her wake. Not a boy, exactly. But not a man either. He doesn't touch her but mirrors her, watches her for clues as to what he should do. Her younger brother or cousin, we decide, as he orders piña coladas for both of them.

She keeps glancing around the bar, sizing up the men and the plastic tiki decorations. The night's possibilities widen her eyes. We want to make fun of her, but she possesses a certain girlishness that awakens our forgiveness. It's not her fault she's haole.

We turn our attention to the men. The local boys have finally arrived, and they look our way. "You like cruise wit' us?" they ask, and we answer, "What? You tink we come hea fo' talk story wit' you?" They laugh at that. They like our hard to get, and they respond, visiting us in small posses of three or four, clustering around our table. We know they're wondering who they'll pair up with, and that that's what we're deciding, too. Which one of these bruddas, or none at all?

The youngest of the three Aiu boys asks Lani Pogan to dance, and the two of them weave among the tables until they are directly in front of the band. He hangs his head and bounces slightly, feeling the beat, and Lani, in her white dress, winks at the singer. She's the worst flirt of us all, and the most hot-tempered, but that's what we like about her. The eldest Aiu asks Mel Chun to come outside for a smoke, and Mel grabs a pack lying on the table. Even though she grew up in San Francisco, the "healthiest city in the world," she claims, she smokes when she goes out. She goes out a lot, she says, subsisting on Heineken and hamburger patties to make up for a childhood of healthy living. Despite her habits, Mel's body is a ball of hard muscle. After four years of competitive outrigger paddling, she's been accepted by us, become one of us locals.

Another round of li hing mui margaritas and the rest of

us join Lani on the dance floor. Our little tourist is bouncing on her stool, her ponytail swinging to the beat of the
music, while her brother approaches the bar to order
more drinks. Ricky, the bar manager, lowers the house
lights and turns on a pair of blue strobes that pulsate in
time to the drumbeat. Cora Jones raises her hand parallel
with her eyes and wiggles her fingers at Ricky. She calls
this her come-and-get-it wave, but we think it makes her
eye look like squid tentacles are growing from it. Lani
nudges us and laughs. Cora's magic works, though: a minute later Ricky is lining up shot glasses on our table. "And
one fo' you, sista," he says to our tourist, plopping a shot
glass in front of her.

She takes it in a single gulp and smiles at us. "Thanks
for sharing," she says brightly. "I'm Susan." A couple of us
nod and smile back, but Lani ignores Susan completely.
"Cora neva get one fo' her," she says.

Ah, none of us paid, but. On da house, we reply.

Lani doesn't care. "She not one of us, her," she says
loud enough for Susan to hear.

We're studying Susan, wondering how she'll respond.
If she accepts she's an outsider, then perhaps we could
hānai her, bring her into the fold for the night. But if she
doesn't understand, then she's just another haole. She
doesn't talk back to Lani, which wins her some points,
but a few minutes later we overhear her whispering to
her brother: "Everyone talks about aloha here, but it's like

Hawaiians are all pissed off. They live in paradise. What is there to be mad about?"

We look at each other, and we feel the heat rising in our faces. Our families are barely affording a life here, the land is being eaten away by developers, the old sugar companies still control water rights. Not only does paradise no longer belong to us, but we have to watch foreigners destroy it. We have plenty aloha for someone who appreciates. We have none for a girl like this. Lani stands like she's about to give a lecture or pop Susan one in the face—which for Lani might be the same thing—but we make her sit down. *Not wort' da trouble,* we say, and for once Lani lets it go.

On the dance floor, Mel has abandoned the elder Aiu and is looking tight with a new guy. We watch them, wondering who he is. He's not a local boy—his skin is too fair, his hair too short—but he doesn't seem straight haole either. He has a solid tan, and he navigates the bar like he's cruised here before. He touches Mel gently on the shoulder, as if to draw her close to him, or just to feel her skin, and us girls raise an eyebrow. We don't like how close he's getting to her before we know who he is.

His hair is shaved close to the scalp, and he dances with the stiffness of a military man. Cora guesses Navy. Lani says Air Force. We watch him raise his arms as if to rest a lei upon Mel's shoulders, and she looks up at him, smiling. He clasps his hands at the back of her neck and bends his knees slightly to look her full in the face. Mel swirls her hips against his, and when a blue strobe illuminates them, we see, on the underside of his right wrist, a tattoo of a mask with tears.

"He's an actor," Cora says excitedly. Cora is majoring in theater at University of Hawai'i. She's our group's academic. "His tattoo is the Greek tragedy mask."

Lani shakes her head. "Da lef' wrist, like look." Just above his watch we glimpse another mask, this one unmarred by tears and wearing a smile.

"Comedy," Cora says, but the rest of us shake our heads. Cora grew up in Kailua. She can be so naive sometimes.

"Smile now, cry later," Lani says.

Prison, the rest of us explain. *Prison ink.*

Cora's face turns pink. "We should go get her."

Lani shrugs as if she doesn't care. She's a Nānākuli girl and likes to pretend she's tougher than the rest of us. But we know better. Whether someone claims Mākaha or Waimānalo or Wahiawa, once they move to town, they lose some of their edge. These days Lani would never play with men headed to or coming from prison.

Cora starts to march toward the dance floor, but we stop her. *Let Lani handle dis,* we say. Cora isn't known for her subtlety. Lani, however, is a master. She sidles up next to Mel and her man and makes like all three of them are going to dance together. We can tell he's pleased with this turn of events by the way he spreads open his arms and hands, as if to embrace both women, a world of women.

Mel shoots us a confused look over her shoulder, and with a little jerk of our heads, we tell her to come back to the table. But she has no chance to act on her own. By the time she returns her gaze to the dance floor, Lani has already nudged her into a crowd of our friends—the Aiu boys and some of the band's crew—and then pushed her along to us.

"Why make me leave?" Mel asks.

"'Cause I neva like yoa taste in men," Lani shoots back, and we laugh.

Mel glances at the dance floor, where her partner is looking for her. "Bryan seemed sweet," she says. "He moved here from California like me."

We shake our heads. We can't believe this guy already has a name. "Did Bryan tell you what he was in prison for?" Cora asks.

"Prison?" Mel says. "I don't think so." We tell her about the ink. She tries to protest but she knows we're telling the truth.

Kaila Ka'awa, whose two brothers have spent most of their lives in and out of county jail, defends Bryan. "You neva know. Could be nutting serious. Jus' borrow one car, yeah."

"You mean steal a car?" Cora says.

"I mean borrow," Kaila says. "But fo'eva. And neva leave one note."

We crack up at that, even Mel, and she thanks us for looking out for her. That's what we do, we tell her. That's what any girls would do. We watch out, we keep each other safe. Maybe he's a good guy, but no sense taking that chance, you know? He's not one of the guys we cruise with, not a local boy. So no worries. We didn't offend anyone important.

The band goes on a break, except for the bassist, who pulls out a guitar polished to a brilliant shine. The bassist is a haole boy, blond as his guitar, with a round, freckled face. He doesn't look legal drinking age. He barely looks old enough to smoke, and Lani sneers, "Tink he one mean guitarist. Like play some emo shit I bet." Haole Boy takes his time tuning the guitar, loosening the higher strings and humming slightly to himself. Lani looks around for Ricky to ask for the bill, but Kaila is watching our bassist-turned-guitarist carefully. Her father plays everything from uke to guitar to drums, and he dances, too, so she knows this scene well. When Kaila pays attention to a performer, we all do.

At last, our haole strums his open strings, and Kaila laughs to herself. "Ho, Haole Boy tune G wahine? He like play slack?" She shakes her head, as if this is the last thing she thought she'd ever see, and she pulls on Lani's dress to make her sit down.

The guitarist takes a deep breath, and then his fingers are flying across the strings. He plays "Whee Ha Swing" like he's Sonny Chillingworth reincarnated, chords and single notes blending tight, so clean and layered that when we close our eyes, we think two guitarists must be onstage. Lani is watching him. When he takes the tempo up, she shivers with pleasure. "Dat boy is mean," Kaila whispers.

"That boy is local," Cora agrees.

"No," Lani says. "Dat boy is one kanaka." At this, we laugh. Lani has paid her highest compliment. She has called him Hawaiian.

We continue to watch the guitarist, his fingers jumping quick as fleas, but out of the corners of our eyes we also notice Bryan approach Susan. He leans his elbows on her table and pulls teasingly at her brother's hat, like he's family, an older cousin or uncle. Susan giggles, and in the blue light, her maroon dress turns a deep purple. "Not everyone can be local," Cora says, motioning toward Susan before returning her attention to the guitarist.

Bryan pulls up a stool and sits between Susan and her brother. He rests a hand on Susan's arm, and she laughs at something he's said, reaching up to graze his cheek with her fingers. Her brother laughs, too, encouraging Bryan to tell another story. Bryan shakes his head and makes a motion like he wants to smoke. The brother pulls a pack from his pocket, but Bryan shakes his head again. He leans close to the table and whispers a secret. We can guess what he's proposing.

Our slack-key guitarist finishes with a smile and ducks his head in humility. "Mahalo nui loa," he murmurs into the microphone. "I thank my uncles Bill and Nahele for giving me this gift I share with you." We bow our heads, too, in reverence to this boy's uncles, his kumu. Yeah, he is one of us, honoring his kūpuna and making his people proud. We respect that.

During the break we head to the restroom, and Susan is there, applying makeup in the mirror. We look at each other, wondering if we should speak to her about Bryan or let her find out by herself. The bathroom is small, slightly cramped, but we all remain, taking turns in the stalls, washing our hands, combing our fingers through our hair, staring at the prints of hula girls hanging on the wall. Finally, we are finished. No more hands can be washed, no more hair adjusted. Lani leans against the door, about to open it, about to leave, when Kaila says to Susan, "Hey, Sista, not my place, but. Da guy you wit' has prison tatts."

"I know." Susan says, speaking to us through the mirror. Her reflection looks at Kaila's. "He told me all about it. He got out two weeks ago."

Kaila raises her eyebrows.

Susan laughs lightly. "Don't worry. He was just in for dealing pot. You know how it is: wrong place, wrong time."

"Jus' be careful," Kaila says. She turns and faces Susan. "You no know him. Yoa brudda no know him."

"You girls really don't want visitors to have a good time, do you?" Susan shrugs. "Whatevs." With a tight smile, she snaps her purse shut and brushes past Lani. The bathroom door swings in Susan's wake, and we are all left staring at the empty space.

Our final toast is to Kiana's promotion at the *Advertiser,* and we drain our glasses. "How did it get so late?" she asks. The clock on Bar Ambrosia's wall insists it's one in the morning.

How did we drink so much? How did we laugh so hard? We feel loose and giggly, the way we always feel after a night together.

"How did this bar get so—" Esther pauses, palms up-turned as if waiting for an answer from heaven. We study the orange walls, the stainless steel tables, the plasma televisions, the chrome salt and pepper shakers.

"Vegas?" Laura suggests.

"MoMA in New York," Kiana says.

Modern. Moneyed. Mainland. We take turns adding adjectives.

"This bar is anything but local," Paula Gilbert agrees. Paula is the only one of us who's never lived off island, never left for college. She is the most local of all of us. Paula is also the only one who is married; she has a two-year-old baby boy and is six months pregnant with a girl. In rare moments, we feel a certain jealousy of her.

As a police officer, Paula manages the rookies as they leave the academy for their stints in Waikīkī. Years ago, she asked to be placed elsewhere—Makiki, Kāhala, even downtown—but now she is resigned to her steady flow of rookies and accepts that Waikīkī is her beat, her training ground and her kingdom. This resignation we view with both scorn and envy. We can't understand how Paula can accept her inferior posting, yet we wish that we, too, could be content with what we've already attained. Perhaps then we'd have the husband and the babies and the home. Perhaps then we'd have more than our careers and our selves.

"Anything but local," Laura repeats. "That's why I come here." We nod our heads in agreement. Here, no tiki decorations hang on the wall. Piña coladas and mai tais are replaced with Manhattans. Reality in space-age pepper shakers.

"Ain't no Lava Lounge, ladies," Esther says.

"Thank goodness we've graduated from that place," Kiana chimes in. We laugh as we remember our days there.

How old is that place? We ask ourselves. *Been around forever. Since before we left for college.*

"Remember the time Esther's brother was working his first beat as a rookie?" Kiana looks slyly at Esther, and we wait for the punchline, laughing before she says it. "And who comes out of Lava Lounge so drunk she can't see straight but his baby sister!"

"And who's the big attorney now," Laura teases.

Esther hangs her head in mock shame. "Yeah, well, remember when Paula met Jason there?"

"Oh God, that *is* how we met," Paula says. "I sometimes forget. He and I told our parents we met in church." She sends us into fresh laughter. Jason and Paula met the July before the rest of us went into our senior year of college. Paula had just earned her associate's degree from Honolulu Community. She was already talking about settling down and starting a family, already setting herself apart from us as we set our sights on mainland jobs and graduate programs.

Our voices echo as we leave the hotel bar. In the lobby, we pause to check that we have house keys and sweaters, that no one has to use the restroom, that no one forgot a cell phone or purse. We are standing in the hotel lobby saying our goodbyes when a couple staggers through the front entrance. We can hear the woman's voice—loud and authoritative—describing a club she visited in Los Angeles. For a moment we study her and the man she's with: he has high cheekbones and olive skin, full lips, extraordinarily tiny ears; she has a ski-jump nose. We remember the nose. She's the girl from the ABC Store. Her brother joins them in the elevator. The door closes, and we look back at each other.

"Oh, to be young again," Laura says lightly.

We kiss each other on the cheek and promise it won't be so long till next time. Paula reminds us that her baby shower is in one month. "And men are welcome, so bring your boyfriends!" she adds cheerfully.

"I think you got the last good one!" Kiana means to sound playful, but a rough edge finds itself in her voice. How do we admit that finding a man who is as successful and as driven and as single as we are is not an easy task?

Paula chuckles humbly. "Oh, no. Plenty other Jasons where I found mine."

"At the Lava Lounge?" Laura asks. We start laughing again. We pause only when the smell of pakalolo wafts over us. We look around the lobby, and the young woman's brother is already back. His eyes are round and red. We look at each other, eyebrows raised.

"Wonder where he got that from," Esther says.

"I should probably arrest him," Paula says, sticking her hands in her pockets. "But I'm off duty right now." We watch him slink through the front entrance toward Kalākaua Avenue.

"Where's his sister?" Laura asks.

Esther glances around the empty lobby. "She must still be upstairs."

Paula frowns. "I hope she knows that man she's with really well."

"Probably just met him tonight," Kiana says drily. "I guess that's the point of vacation."

The party begins to break up. Paula offers a ride home to Laura and a couple of others who live on Diamond Head, and they leave. Kiana and Esther linger with the rest of us to talk about Paula's baby bump and the steadiness of Jason's job as a photographer. They live in an 'ohana behind his parents' house. With two kids they'll outgrow the tiny cottage in no time, but they'll never be able to afford their own place. We also wonder about Laura's resort design, worried that another development will push housing prices further upward, making it harder still for our people to remain on their land. "And what about water usage?" Esther demands. Even in conversation with us, she turns hot-blooded lawyer when the subject of land rights comes up. But Kiana rests a hand on Esther's shoulder, and the tension dissipates.

We kiss each other on the cheek one last time. We've let another half hour slip by. As we reach the front door, we spot the tourist girl and her date exiting the elevator. They breeze by us, their heads bent together, his right arm thrown protectively around her shoulders. They are heading for the back of the hotel, where the veranda overlooks the ocean. From there they can gain beach access. Leaving the carpeted lobby, she trips and falls to her hands and knees. But she's up again in a second, giggling with embarrassment, and he laughs with her. He slips his arm around her waist and grips her tightly, steering her away from the lobby.

The humid air carries the sound of their voices to us. "Baby," he says. "Watch yourself."

But she's not listening. She just keeps repeating, "This is it. This is paradise."

They descend the stairs of the veranda and cross the patio. Her body pitches forward as she walks as if she's in a state of perpetual freefall.

As we drive home, we think of nothing but her words.

❦

"Like go home now?" Cora asks us. We are standing outside the Lava Lounge, the music still ringing in our ears and the trade winds cooling our damp skin. It's nearly two in the morning.

"Can surf early tomorrow," Lani says. "Mean da swell, yeah." Australia's eastern coast has seen record storm activity in the past week, and the newscasters claim that the weather system is finally headed north. We're giddy with the promise of six-foot faces on the south shore.

"Let's check the water before we head home," Mel suggests.

We leave behind the club and Kūhiō Avenue, with its explosion of car horns and police sirens, men hawking coupons for an indoor shooting range—half off for women!—and prostitutes whispering "Aloha" in lilting voices. When we reach the beach, the night is suddenly quiet, and we breathe deeply of the salt air. In the distance, the waves at Pops are gilded by moonlight, and we watch them rise and lumber along, slow and unambitious. By the morning we want them stacking up clean and high.

We pause outside the Banyan Hotel, the warm light from the lobby casting our shadows across the water's edge. The tide sucks at the sand beneath our toes like a vacuum. We look into the hotel, and we can almost understand why here, in Waikīkī, the world appears perfect. The hotel lobbies are brimming with flower arrangements and sticky with the scent of ginger. The island air is warm and heavy as a blanket. And the people are beautiful. Tan and healthy, with muscles carved from koa wood and cheeks the color of strawberry guava. These people—our people—look fresh as cut fruit, ready to be caressed, to be admired. These are people to be trusted. This is not New York or Los Angeles. No, Hawai'i is heaven. A dream.

Not far from us, we hear someone moan, and we giggle. A girl says, "No," and we take a step in the direction of the voice. But her husky voice is muffled, and in the next moment we think we hear an excited "Oh." We stop. We see this all the time. Tourist couples think the beach is some private fantasy island. Like no one can see them out there, when they're about as hidden from view as mating monk seals. How many times have we glimpsed naked ass, white as moonlight, pumping away for all it's worth?

We think of all the tourist women who have come here and taken a man to bed with them—or the men who have taken women. Are they proud of themselves, these tourists? Do they feel they've acquired the most exotic souvenir, or that they are now true islanders?

Our mood gets heavy fast. We tell each other to loosen up. Tomorrow the surf will be high and we'll wash away all these questions in the water. We start to walk back to the street. We pause when we hear splashing nearby and a small, thrilled shriek, but when we look down the beach all we see are shadows staining the sand.

⟋

For the first time since we were college kids, we dream of the rolling ocean. Not of boardrooms or courtrooms, classrooms or meeting rooms, but of waves, of *room*, as much as we can bear, and the space of the sea. We dream we are falling deep into the ocean. At first the water is warm, comforting even, but suddenly we are scared. We can't find our way up or out. We need air, and none exists beneath the weight of all this water. We hear a woman screaming for help, and we're not sure if the voice is ours or someone else's.

When we awake, our quilts are kicked to the foot of our beds. Kiana has balled her sheet in her hand. Esther's pillowcase is clammy with sweat. Jason takes Paula in his arms, presses her tear-dampened face to his shoulder, and tells her that everything will be okay.

But we don't think everything is okay. Something is amiss, muddled. Years have passed since we listened to our dreams, since we were youthful enough to trust them. Now we take the time to hear ourselves. In the quiet of our bedrooms, we finally fall back asleep, but we remain just below the surface of waking, afraid to again sink completely into sleep.

⟋

We're on the early shift again, so we arrive at five in the morning. We begin by dusting the surfaces in the lobby, vacuuming up the sand guests have tracked in, sweeping the patio—which the busboys for the Banyan Bar will later sweep again—and polishing all the metal fixtures and lampshades. The front desk signs the delivery slip for the arrangement of birds of paradise and centers the vase on the round wooden table in the middle of the lobby. Always birds of paradise, their pointed beaks threatening to stab the first woman who tries to dust the table. Today the stems are unusually long, and the flower heads sink wearily.

As soon as we finish with the common areas, we are supposed to load our room carts and ride the elevator to our assigned floors. But first we always slip away to glimpse the ocean in the first rays of sunlight. The sky is still dark in the west, but the horizon near Diamond Head is blooming with a pale yellow light. We cross the veranda, drawn by this soft glow, and descend to the patio. Even though we are facing east, toward mainland America, we pretend that in the distance, beyond the white haze that hangs above the ocean, lie our home islands. We don't like to think of ourselves as homesick, but sometimes we feel an ache for their still, quiet air.

We kneel to roll a few grains of sand between our fingers. Here, the sand is soft and fine, imported from beaches on Maui and Kaua'i. This sand feels fake to us, unlike the coarser sand of our islands, the sand that, like us, is whole and hardened. We stand and glance up again at the horizon, admire the white-yellow of the sky, and this is when we see her.

She is lying on her side, her right arm tucked beneath her ear, her back turned to us. People sleep out on this beach all the time: drifters, druggies, drunks, runaways, lovers, and tourists too lost or high to care if they make it back to their hotels. We're not sure if we should disturb her, but something in the absolute stillness of her body makes us move toward her. Up close, we see that her hair is stringy and wet, and her dress hem has slid halfway up her left butt cheek. Stassi Nifon tugs on the hem to cover her nakedness, but we are still embarrassed for the girl.

We lean over her and place our hands on the wet cotton of her dress. We shake her gently. "Wake up," we tell her. "It's morning." She doesn't stir. She is heavy in our hands. We command her to get up, to move, but she doesn't listen. When we touch her bare arm, her skin is cold. We jump away from her, startled. Her skin is too cold.

A couple of us run to tell management. Those who hesitated to leave the patio now retreat to the housekeeping office, not wishing to be involved. But those who found her, who touched her, who recognize her—we stay. We form a circle around her, protecting her even though she is beyond our protection. When management comes running to verify the police are needed, we remain where we are. Our shift leader tells us to go back inside, but we ignore her. Management withdraws to the hotel.

The girl's hair and skin are pale as the sky at sunrise. She is older than even our eldest girls, and, on any other day, we could have called her *haole,* foreigner, a white woman independent and capable of caring for herself. But in these few minutes before the police come running down the beach with a first-aid kit and walkie-talkie, this girl is a child. She is helpless. She is in need of a mother, and that's a job at which we are experts. The sky lightens in the west to a dull blue as flares of orange rip the eastern sky. *We are here,* we tell the unmoving girl. *All us mothers are here.*

We've just turned the corner at the snack stand when we spot the crowd gathered outside of the Banyan Hotel. "Can jus' surf Canoes," Lani says, pointing to the break in front of us. "No crowd dere yet."

"Bet it's a turtle on the beach," Cora yawns. She presses the heel of her palm to her left temple. We're all a little ragged this morning, from lack of sleep and one too many margaritas. "Turtles always bring out the tourists. No one's in the water." We cross the sand, its cold granules clumping between our toes.

As we draw closer to the crowd, we see police uniforms and hear the odd burst of voice and crackled silence particular to walkie-talkies. The hotel's housekeeping staff, identifiable by their floral-patterned dresses and white tennis shoes, are taking turns being interviewed by a couple of officers. When each interview is complete, the women are pointed in the direction of the hotel, but they refuse to leave the beach. Instead, they return in silence to the circle their compatriots have formed. The women stand sentinel, very still and very tall. A man in a black windbreaker tries to take photographs of whatever is inside their circle, but each time he asks the housekeeping women to move or attempts to nudge them aside, they block his way. Finally, he gives up and takes his photos in the narrow spaces between the women's bodies. We're past the the hotel's patio before we realize the back of the photographer's jacket reads "Coroner's Office."

Mel turns to one of the housekeepers and asks quietly, "Auntie, what happened?"

The woman glances toward the ground shaking her head, and we glimpse a maroon dress, white legs, a half-closed hand. We run to the other side of the circle to see the face, and even when the police yell, "'Ey, get 'em outta hea!" we refuse to budge.

Lani, as always, is the first to speak. "We know her," she says. Her voice is heavy with wonder and shock.

We know her, we repeat. We know her and we warned her and we saw him. Cora shakes her head in disbelief. Mel looks sick.

The police officers frown at us in disbelief or annoyance, but one of them, a petite woman with dark skin and a protruding belly, yells at the rest, "Why are you staring at them? Do something." She's older than the other officers, and they defer to her. At first, they tell us to pile our boards on the sand and not go anywhere, but then they wander away to watch the coroner or manage the growing crowd. A couple of us sigh heavily and we stare out at Pops. We'll miss dawn patrol, we think. And then we're ashamed for being so crass. We'd like to turn off our minds. We'd like to think only of Susan, of her smile when she thanked us for the drink, of the eagerness in her eyes. We'd like to cry, if for no other reason than to prove to ourselves that we are empathetic humans, but we have no tears for her. We're already wondering if we'll make it to work on time, what we should eat for lunch, whether the surf will still be good in the afternoon and not blown out by the winds. Already our lives are moving on, forward, into the future, and Susan's life has been left behind on this beach.

The policewoman follows our gaze with her eyes and watches the waves with us. For a moment, we're all looking at the ocean with the same longing, the same sense of hurling through time and space. She approaches us. "If we talk now, you all should still have time for a short session," she whispers, smiling gently.

We relax. We can trust her. We'll make it into the ocean after all. With sudden clarity, we remember hearing splashing in the water the night before and a woman's scream. We hadn't thought it anything more than a shriek of laughter.

"I tink we heard one scream last night," Cora begins. At the same moment, Lani cuts in with "She neva like listen."

The policewoman pulls out a pad of paper. She looks at all of us at once. "Girls, let's start at the beginning."

By the time Paula conference calls us on our office lines we've already watched the early news. We tell her the police sketch looks just like him, that man with Susan. We have learned the girl's name and now we use it. Susan. It makes us feel as if we're helping her.

Paula tells us a group of surfer girls contributed to the artist's sketch, which Paula personally approved. "Just like how we saw him," she says, echoing the rest of us. Her voice is hollow over the phone, and we know what she's thinking: We're older and more experienced than the Susans of the world. We're career women. We should have seen that Susan was getting herself into trouble. We should have done something.

"What about the brother?" Kiana asks as if to divert attention from herself, or ourselves.

"He returned to the hotel not long after we all went home," Paula says. "He figured they had gone out to a club or something. He didn't think to go looking for his sister. He felt like, if he gave her space, he was helping her out."

"What was he thinking?" Laura asks.

"He wasn't," Kiana says, sighing.

"If my boy left his sister alone in a hotel room with some . . ." Paula stops herself.

We wonder how many days will pass before someone comes forward with information on the suspect. On an island like ours, a man doesn't run. Can't run. The airlines have his sketches, the ships as well, though we've never heard of a suspect trying to escape via Carnival Cruise Lines. On island, a man has to hide, hunker down, find friends and use them. The question is not how will he be caught, but who will turn him in.

We don't tell each other about our dreams, but we hint at them. *Last night I barely slept,* we say, or *I was awake all night thinking about that girl.* In the early morning, alone in our apartments and condos and houses, when the only sounds were the winds sweeping out of the valleys and a dog barking in the distance, we found ourselves wondering how we escaped those treacherous years of our late teens and early twenties. *We lived in a different time,* we tell each other, and the world suddenly appears fragile and sad.

Esther says Hawai'i is becoming more and more like the mainland, and for once we don't hear anger in her voice, just regret.

But Laura is angry. "If you were in Chicago, would you go home with a man you just met at a bar? Would you trust a stranger with your hotel key in L.A.?"

"If I was young, maybe, and on vacation," Kiana answers.

"How young?" Laura challenges. "This woman, this Susan, she was twenty-two. She should have known better!"

Paula interrupts. "Laura, at that age we hardly knew any better."

"I knew better."

Paula offers a hollow laugh. "I visited you at college. I saw the risks you were willing to take in those days. Inviting guys back to your apartment, getting into cars with friends of friends of friends. You didn't know those guys any better than Susan knew this man."

Laura is quiet.

"Back then we all were that way," Esther says gently. "We were young, naive."

Laura's sadness radiates across the phone lines, and we shiver. "So were we just lucky?"

⁓

Throughout the day we argue over Susan, acting as if we knew her enough to speak for her. Some of us claim she was all over that Bryan at the Lava Lounge. Others say she was too innocent to know what he was really after. Cora tries to find a middle ground: "Maybe she wanted to hook up but didn't want to sleep with him, and he got mad."

We watch the news on television, wanting to know the latest updates. Two hotel security guards are interviewed. They say they saw a couple rolling in the sand. "Two lovers," they claim, but when pressed, they admit it could have been a struggle. "All da time we see tings like dat, but," they tell the reporters. We feel disgust with Security. Why didn't they investigate? Why didn't they interrupt? We think of the noises we heard and we ask ourselves the same questions.

In the late afternoon, we hear that the hotel is going to sponsor a small remembrance ceremony and that more than one hundred people plan on attending, mostly locals. Our community has been shaken. We want to give something, but we don't know what or to whom. Susan's family has already stated, via a lawyer, that they will not be present at the ceremony. They know none of us, so they mourn alone. We feel sorry for them. We are angry at them. When they see local people, they must think we are the ones who brought them death.

Us girls buy white plumeria lei at Safeway and put them around our necks. We meet on the beach in front of the Banyan, but we don't stay for the ceremony. Instead, we paddle out to Pops, past the break and into deep water until we are far from any other surfers. We sit on our boards and form a tight circle, our knees bumping into the rails of the boards on either side of us, and we *pule*, we pray. We ask forgiveness. We ask for patience. We ask for guidance, not only for our lives but also for Susan's family, and for the islands. Then we chew through the strings of our lei and toss each flower into the center of the circle. The strings we tie around our wrists.

We begin the long paddle back to land. The flowers are still there when we glance behind, sunlight reflecting off their white petals like small lanterns on the surface of the water.

By the time we return to shore, the beach is filled again with its usual sunbathers and swimmers. All that's left of the remembrance ceremony is a confused jumble of magenta orchids and red carnations, pale pink roses toppling over green ti leaf, orange birds of paradise sticking out like cheap sparklers. We stand over the pile and look down. The setting sun is hot on the back of our necks, and in the heat all the flowers are wilting.

WANLE

Hawai'i is a cock-pit, on the ground the well-fed cocks fight.
—FROM THE CHANT OF HAUI-KA-LANI

The Indian said "Poi Dog" the way other men say Princess or Babydoll. He always said it real sweet, as if he didn't know the meaning, didn't know a poi dog was a mutt, the kind of dog that finds you and not the kind you breed special. Even in bed, naked and chilled, waiting for the damp air of the valley to rise around us in ghostly mist, he'd whisper, "Poi Dog," and I'd tuck my head beneath his neck to feel his breath hot on my cheek.

I called him the Indian. I didn't mean it bad or good. I just called things what they were, as my father had before me. My dad was the one who named me "Wanle," which he said in Chinese means "It is gone." He claimed, after I was born, his fears left him. "Dey all wen go away," he'd say. "Oh, and yoa mudda. *It* wen go away, too."

Every morning, even before the roosters awoke, the Indian started banging pans around in the kitchen. When I smelled frying eggs, I knew it was time to climb out of bed and fix breakfast for my boys. I measured their food carefully, mashing together a quarter pound of raw ground beef, two chicken eggs, three tablespoons of vitamin powder, and four teaspoons of fish oil for omega-3s. I divided the mixture into two aluminum pie tins and added extra cornmeal to one of the dishes. The cornmeal was to help bulk up my two blacks. My hatches, who fought with their speed and agility rather than brute strength, didn't need any extra weight.

In the yard, my roosters were blinking at me from behind the wooden-slatted walls of their cages. The first two coops belonged to Hapa and Keoni, my prize blacks; Lono and Kū, my hatches, occupied the next two. At the front of each cage was a wooden door, and cut into each door was a square opening just large enough for the birds to poke their heads through. A plastic feed cup hung in front of every hole, and I scraped a portion of the food into each cup. The birds stuck their heads out the door and began to eat. I left promising to exercise them in the afternoon when I returned home from work.

Once the boys were fed, I visited the hen house to collect eggs, pour fresh water in the bowls, and toss feed. I kept hens mostly for the eggs, but also because I hoped the scent of females might keep my boys a little riled, and they needed that extra edge if they were going to win. I always lingered too long with the birds, and the Indian would come out on the back porch, his thermos of coffee in hand, and call me in. "You'll make me late for work again."

I'd toss the last of the seed at the hens and sprint to the back door. No matter how hot the afternoons were destined to become, the mornings were always fresh and damp, and their air soothed me like a drink. "Those cocks are worse competition than the other kind," the Indian laughed.

"Oh, stop it." I smacked him on the 'ōkole, and he bent down to kiss me. The Indian never left for work without kissing me goodbye, and though I sometimes teased him about being soft for me, I wouldn't have wanted it any other way.

After the Indian's truck set off rumbling down Hale-akalā Highway, I showered and dressed. I locked all the doors to the house, though no one else Upcountry bothered to, but my father's habits had stayed with me. The Indian, he never locked anything.

I cooked the breakfast shift at the Pā'ia Diner, return-ing home in the early afternoon to train my birds. I made them run, peck, scratch, and extend their wings. I used the training tricks my father had taught me, and I discovered some of my own. The birds were exercised separately—if left alone, their natural tendency was to fight each other. I worked with my boys until early evening, when the Indian called me into the house to cook dinner, and then I nestled the birds in their cages for the night.

My dad used to say cockfighting was in his blood: the Chinese in him liked betting, the Hawaiian liked fighting, and the Filipino liked birds. Before he died, my dad raised some of the most aggressive, well-trained battlecocks on the islands. His birds never lost a fight, so he made plenty of money off his roosters. He provided security at the fights, too, didn't have an allegiance to one boss or another, and wasn't asked to. The bosses only expected him to stay honest, and stay quiet, and he said no problem, he could do both.

My father treated his birds like children, allowing them to eat inside the house or inviting them to ride with him in his truck. He trusted his birds more than he did my grandmother or uncle. My dad's favorite black, 'Ono, slept at the foot of his bed. "My guard dog, him," my dad claimed. "'Ono like tell me if someone try kill me." He told me that between his birds and my mom, he had chosen the birds. He said one day I'd have to make the same choice, and I'd do as he had, with the same result.

When I turned sixteen, my father gave me my first rooster to raise and train myself. The bird was a hatch,

and I named him Makana, which in Hawaiian means "gift."
My dad showed me how to hold Makana's feet and beak
so the bird wouldn't attack, and how to hum to calm him.
More importantly, I learned how to make Makana into a
better fighter. In the yard, I'd come at him with my hand
wrapped in a sparring glove, back him into corners, wave
a feather duster in his face, flip him on his back, and watch
him right himself. Makana needed to feel both threatened
and capable, afraid enough to fight but not so scared he'd
flee. Sometimes I emerged with a bloodied arm, my skin
bearing deep lines where his beak had found me, but I became used to this. It was all part of being a pitter.

"You tink I be good like you, Dad?" I asked my father
one day in the yard. In those days I spoke pidgin without
thinking of it, not switching for one person or another,
not even for my teachers in school. I had my father's way
with words, which was to say, I didn't consider them.

My father looked down at Makana, who was on a leash
at my feet scratching lazily at the ground. Next my father
looked up at me, and then at the bird again. I gave the leash
a gentle tug and Makana stopped scratching. He cocked
his head up at me, and his eyes were clear and intelligent.
He was waiting for a command. When I whistled low and
soft, he walked in a wide circle beside me, his head pumping in and out, his talons kicking behind his tail. He was
looking for an opponent.

My dad laughed. "Yeah, girl," he said, resting a hand
on my shoulder. "You make one fine pitta. Like da papa."

In the front of the house a car backfired. My dad froze, watching the street. For a moment the air was still, but then the usual noises returned: a dog barked, the wind squealed up the mountain, the mynahs cawed in the monkeypod trees. My dad relaxed, and I released the breath I had been holding without realizing it. But Makana remained unsettled by the sharp noise, and he wouldn't stop squawking. When my dad reached for the bird, I tugged the leash toward me.

"Can take care of it," I said. I took Makana in my arms and hummed, pressing his head beneath my chin so he could feel the vibration of my vocal cords. He sank into my arms.

"Jus' like da dad, you." My father kissed me on the forehead. "Like make me proud. Make me know you always take care da papa. Always take care tings fo' me."

I didn't know then what my father meant by things, but later, after he was killed, I began to understand.

That summer after my father died, the heat came early. The birds molted sooner in the season, and in the evenings, instead of training, I walked through the high grass behind my uncle's house in Makawao. I stayed out until the sky was dark, and the huge boulders littering the pastureland appeared like the backs of ancient gods, curled up and sleeping. This is how I found the Indian—when the sky was purple and the earth was still hot from the sun beating into it.

The Indian lived Upcountry because he liked the slower pace of life. He worked construction, but he took classes at Maui Community. "To keep my mind sharp," he said, and I wondered why with a body like his he felt he needed a sharp mind. He confided that he wanted to take a poetry class. He practiced Buddhism. He was considering becoming a vegetarian. Sometimes I laughed when he told me things like these. I didn't know anyone who was a vegetarian.

For all his funny notions, the Indian still knew how to be a man. He had a way of walking into a bar with his hand on my lower back that told everyone I belonged to him. If some haole kid gave me lip, the Indian would rise to his full height, his shoulder blades pressed back until they nearly touched, and his hands curled into fists that pulsed as he squeezed his fingers into his palms.

The Indian never fought anyone. He never needed to. I used to tell him, "If someone really push you, you gon swing." The Indian always disagreed. He had grown up with a father who fought easily, and he'd left South Dakota to avoid that inheritance.

"What if someone like go at you first?" I once asked. "Or what if dey come afta me?"

"Come after." The Indian emphasized the "r" sound. He had grown up on rez English, with its own cadences and slang, but now that we were together he wanted both of us to use what he considered proper English. This was just another one of the Indian's self-imposed limits. As with language, his gentlemanliness seemed to abide by a set of invisible expectations.

"Come after," I repeated.

"In answer to your question, I would walk away."

"What if I hit you? Like, right now, I jus' hit you."

The Indian laughed. "I would never hit back. Never."

"What if I ignore you for one whole week? How you like get my attention?"

The Indian ran his finger along the side of my body, from just beneath my armpit to my hip, and then he reached around and squeezed my 'ōkole. "I have plenty of ways of getting your attention."

I laughed when he said sweet words like those, and I understood that beneath them he meant what he said. He was not one to waste words or use them lightly, as I often did. In bed, clasping the Indian's naked body to mine, I could see the map of his father's attentions: a broken nose that now veered slightly to the right, deep cuts that had healed pale and thin, marks from a belt where the skin had furled into itself and thickened. "I'll never be like him," the Indian promised, and I believed him.

The way Uncle Lee told it, Mr. Oh had wanted to rise in the ranks, and security was the next logical job for him.

My dad, however, had a corner on that market, and the bosses trusted him. Mr. Oh wasn't the one who killed my father, but he told stories to the bosses on O'ahu, and as my dad used to say, talking is as good as pulling a trigger.

After my father's death, I moved in with Uncle Lee. My grandmother wanted me to live with her. She knew Uncle Lee fought birds, and she didn't want me getting mixed up in all that, but I was eighteen and did as I pleased.

Revenge would have been easy. I could have asked my dad's friends to do what I couldn't: send dogs to murder Mr. Oh's birds. And, if I had really wanted to, I probably could have found someone to murder Mr. Oh. But these forms of retribution weren't right by my standards. Mr. Oh wouldn't know who had sent the dogs, and I wanted recognition for settling the score. I wanted that responsibility and that pleasure. What I didn't want was blood on my hands. Maybe Mr. Oh could sleep at night without being haunted by the memory of my father, but I knew I couldn't live with myself if I had caused the death of a man.

It took me six months to figure out how to take my revenge. The idea came to me at a derby in Haiku. Al Chen, one of my dad's buddies, was hosting as he often did. Mr. Oh hovered behind Al throughout the weighing and banding. He watched that Al drew for order and then paired the birds by weight, and that the pairings were truly random. Mr. Oh also demanded that all the bands be tied in front of him to prevent switching. My father had never demanded that the pitters report to him in addition to Al.

The fights didn't go well for my uncle or his buddy Zoo, who lost three hundred dollars and his favorite hatch to one of Mr. Oh's birds. Back in the stands, Zoo's doughy face drooped lower than usual. "I like see someone beat dat man." In the yellow light of the tent I saw brown smears on his forearms where he had forgotten to wash off his bird's blood. "I neva lost when yoa papa was living," he told me.

"Ah well, none us did," Uncle Lee said.

I nodded in agreement. When my father had been alive, he had owned the birds and trained them; Zoo and Uncle Lee just pitted. Now it was different. Now they owned and trained the birds, and the animals lost. I wondered if they followed my father's training regimen, if they fed the birds carefully. They must have been doing something wrong to be losing like they were.

"I t'rough afta tonight." Zoo scowled in the direction of Mr. Oh.

"You say dat now. Tomorrow, but, you like buy anotha bird and stat ova again."

"Jus' for see Mr. Oh lose."

"Yeah, I like see dat man and his birds lose someting big, you know?" My uncle shook his head. "If my brudda stay alive . . ."

I felt my father's absence hanging over all of us, and I wanted to give my uncles what my dad had given them: winning birds, winning bets. "If I wen train my birds right, if I train like my dad, I could beat Mr. Oh."

Zoo looked up from his hands, and his bald spot shone in the lights. "Ah, babe. You good, but. Da dad had plenny help, you know."

"I gon have help. Uncle help me train, and I talk story wit' da gaffers . . ." I stopped talking. Uncle Lee and Zoo were looking at each other. I wondered if they were doubting my abilities as a pitter. "I can do it, you know. I can beat 'im."

"We know, babe," Uncle Lee said. "You gon make us proud. You make yoa papa proud, too."

"We can help 'er plenny," Zoo said, "Al, too."

My uncle shook his head. "No, we let 'er do dis her way." He gave Zoo another look, and Zoo bowed his head. What understanding had passed between them I didn't know.

After that night, Uncle Lee distanced himself from me. He helped me train when we were at his house, but he wouldn't assist me at the fights because he said I needed to be seen as independent. I spent more time observing the other pitters: how they prepped their birds, how they taught them to move, how they chose their gaffers, and what kind of gaffs they used. The gaffers wouldn't out-and-out teach me how to tie, but they let me watch, and I started to learn which knives responded best to which style of tying.

That fall, I mostly watched my birds lose—maybe not lose the fight, but lose an eye, a toe, a swath of golden-red feathers. Those that won the fight might heal and two weeks later be back in the ring, but the ones that lost I killed with a quick knife to their throats. Makana went this way. A lot of good birds did.

I wasn't looking to win. I was looking to understand why certain birds lost. Often, the bird that lost was the one that appeared strongest at the start. It moved fast, lifted its wings in an attempt to intimidate, came at its opponent with its claws, even aimed a few well-placed pecks in the vicinity of the other bird's face. By contrast, the winning cocks were usually less immediately aggressive. They hung back for a few seconds, appeared to assess the ring, and waited for their opponent to make the first move. Then, rather than threaten, the slow starter went for the kill. They didn't bother with claws and pecking. They knew how to use the knife.

In December, when the derby season drew to a close, I returned to visiting the Indian more often. He had so much he wanted to teach me: how to drive stick shift, how to shoot a gun, how to circle my hips when I was on top in bed. For Christmas he built me a hen house, and I moved in with him.

The Indian started the poetry class he wanted to take. On Sunday mornings, lying in our bed, the sheets crumpled like paper around our knees and thighs, I watched him write. "There's nothing complicated in poetry," he told me. "Like this I just wrote: 'Chickens scratch the dirt/Looking for feed I pluck eggs/Dawn's sun cracks open.' "

I thought of what I would write about my father or my mom leaving or the roosters, but I never knew what to say.

"Just write what it feels like to be alive," the Indian instructed. He tore a sheet of paper from his spiral-bound notebook and handed it to me. "Like Bashō says: a poet must know the ordinary feelings of an ordinary life. Write about the quotidian."

"I don't know what that means."

"Daily. Regularly."

I looked down at the piece of paper in my lap. *I daily train my birds*, I wrote. *I regularly miss my dad.*

"That's not really what I had in mind." The Indian handed me a new piece of paper. "Try writing about something beautiful in your life instead."

Lono's tail feathers are red like lava.

"Or write something that puts you at peace and in harmony with the world."

I stared at the paper. "I don't know what makes me feel peace. Feeding the birds, I guess. Or walking them. I feel at peace when I see them on their teepees."

"What about me? Don't I put you at peace?"

I studied him. His short, black hair was silvering slightly at the temples, and his jowls had taken on a little weight during the holidays. Still, looking at him made my heart leap. I wanted to tell him that he excited me. I felt the world spin hotter and faster when he touched me. I felt the opposite of peace. But instead of explaining all this, I just said, "No. Not at peace."

"You love those birds more than me, that's why." He snapped shut his notebook and tossed it on the floor.

"I mean, you do put me at peace sometimes."

"You just said I don't."

"You do. Believe me."

"I wish I could believe you, but I don't think a life can be peaceful when it's focused on fighting."

"Jus' 'cause I fight birds doesn't mean I'm not at peace."

"What about your dad?"

"I have peace with my dad."

"That's not what I mean. Ask yourself: was your dad at peace? From what you tell me, the fights ruled his life. And yours."

"It never was like that. He had no fears, no regrets. He lived his life how he wanted to live it. I'm not angry 'bout it."

"Then why do you want to fight Mr. Oh so badly?"

"I can be at peace with my dad and still want revenge for what Mr. Oh did."

"That's impossible." He shook his head. His eyes looked tired and sad. "It's like you want to do what your dad didn't finish. Like you don't even know who you are. Are you your father or yourself? You don't know."

I rested my forehead against his. His eyelashes were thick and long, and in the corner of his left eye a yellow crust of sleep clung to his skin. I kissed him long and hard, and his tongue searched for mine. We kept our eyes open. I wanted him to see all of who I was. "I know who I am."

"Do you?" he whispered. He climbed on me, and the weight of his body pressed all the air from my lungs. I tipped my hips up toward his. "Tell me then: Are you a fighter or a lover?"

"Lover."

He kissed me hard on the mouth, and I felt myself grow wet. "Are you your father's girl or my woman?"

"Your woman."

His hand slipped beneath the elastic of my panties and tugged them to my knees. He was hard against my thigh. "Are you a rooster or a poi dog?"

"Poi dog," I whispered.

"Good girl," he said and entered me.

At the end of the spring, as the Indian's first poetry class drew to a close, he came to me in the yard. "Our crew won the hotel bid in Wailea."

"Das good," I said absently. I was trying to teach Hapa how to circle on command, as Makana had once done. Hapa was at the point where he recognized the whistle but didn't make full turns yet. "You won't have to leave for work so early in the morning."

"Maybe you and I can spend a little more time in bed then." He reached around me and rested his hands on my breasts.

I looked up from Hapa and laughed. "Can. Remember, but, you are my alarm clock. You tell me when it's time to wake the boys." I kissed the Indian on the ear and then stepped out of his embrace. I leaned over Hapa again and gave a low whistle. When he paused halfway through the circle, I patted the underside of his tail feathers and he completed the turn. "Ho, see that? He's going to be ready for the fall derbies." I rewarded Hapa with a handful of feed and a soft coo.

"The derbies . . ." The Indian's voice trailed off. "Are you going to spend this fall fighting again? I thought maybe now that we're living together . . ."

"I'm not going to fight every weekend. Just a couple big ones."

"I never saw you last fall." The Indian folded his arms across his chest. "I don't want you fighting those birds anymore."

"I don't see what you think is wrong with entering a couple derbies." I picked up Hapa. The day's lesson was over.

"I don't like the violence."

I stroked Hapa's hackle, which calmed him before bed like a glass of warm milk does a child. "You watch boxing and MMA. That's violent."

The Indian rested his hands on the crown of his head, a habit he had developed when he was frustrated with a poem. "It's not the same. And anyway, I don't trust the men."

"Those men are uncles. They're always looking out for me." I nuzzled Hapa and then settled him in his coop. Beyond the cages the valley was gold in the evening light.

The Indian frowned, and the silence between us stretched long and thin. He was the kind of man comfortable with stillness, and just when you began to think he forgot you were beside him, he'd speak. "You don't act like a lady when you're at the fights."

I laughed at him. I couldn't help it. "When do I ever act like a lady? I always been a tita and always will be. If you like be with a lady, then go find one māhū."

He rolled his fingers into his palms and squeezed. "I don't like the fights is all," he repeated. "I don't like what your dad was."

"What does that mean?"

"I hear things, you know."

"What kine things?"

"It doesn't matter. What matters is I don't like what the fighting does to people. Especially you."

"What does it do to me?" My voice rose.

"It makes you something you're not. Something hard and mean and vengeful."

"Maybe that's exactly what I am."

"No." He shook his head, his anger choking him. "You're not. You can't be." He turned away from me then and stalked back to the house.

I stayed outside with my birds until the sun sank completely into the ocean. The valley below turned purple in the reflected light, and above me Haleakalā became nothing more than a black shadow against a black sky. I wanted to please the Indian, wanted to be the woman he thought I should be, but the roosters were my dad. They were my way of doing right by him, and they were me.

For the next week, as soon as the Indian returned home from work, he took to the rolling hills beyond our yard. He'd walk for hours across the rocky fields, disappearing into the tall, green grass like a fish diving into deep water. For seven nights I ate alone when evening came and slept alone, too. He camped out on the couch in the living room, and silence reigned in our house. I didn't rush him to speak nor did I ask for forgiveness. Instead, I continued with my routine, with the birds, with my studies and my plans for beating Mr. Oh. Then, on the eighth morning, I awoke, and the Indian had fastened a poem to the bathroom mirror:

> *In autumn evening*
> *a traveler alone walks*
> *a long silent road.*

I didn't know what the poem meant, but I didn't ask him for answers. I simply tucked his note away in my underwear drawer, where I kept other scraps of his artistry, and found myself thinking about autumn in May.

That night, the Indian waited for me in bed. I took my time undressing in the corner of the bedroom. I pulled off my socks, brown with mud from hosing down the hen house, and dumped them in the laundry hamper along with my jeans. "Hey, Poi Dog," the Indian said, like he was getting my attention. I knew what he wanted. He was asking me to slow down, take my time, take his time.

I turned my back to him and slid my tank top over my head, letting him watch my shoulder blades sharpen and retreat. I allowed him to glimpse my bare neck before I untied my hair and let it fall, dusty and tangled, across my back. I slipped my arms out of my bra straps, let the bra fall to the floor softly, like sand falling on sand.

"Come here," he whispered. I didn't want him to say he was sorry or that he missed me or that he forgave me. I didn't want him to say anything. I walked toward him, my arms crossed over my breasts, stopping just short of the bed and refusing to move. Finally, he reached up his hands and pulled me on top of him.

A week later news came that Mr. Oh would be competing in the big derby in Makawao on the second weekend of September. I told Uncle Lee I would enter, and I told him to make sure Mr. Oh knew. I didn't tell the Indian anything about any of it.

The Indian and I didn't talk about my birds, and I trained them only when he wasn't home. Still, their presence hovered between us. He stopped eating eggs, a small protest I was forced to accept, and began spending more evenings out of the house, playing poker with his friends, sometimes drinking.

A part of me wanted to stop with the birds. As June came to a close and the vog settled heavy in the valley, I began telling myself I could walk away. That I wanted the Indian more than I wanted revenge.

The night was one where the air is fixed, and the summer heat covers you heavy as the ocean until all you recognize in the world is the smell of your own sweat. I fell asleep early, the Indian next to me, both of us so exhausted we felt drugged. At around two in the morning I started suddenly and sat up in bed. The Indian was sleeping, his back to me, the sheets covering nothing but his ankles.

The house was still, but somewhere beyond the silence, beyond the sensation of being alone in a world thick with moisture, I heard noise. The sound was sharp and hollow, like an ax on metal, and it was followed by a muffled shuffling. I thought immediately of my birds. "Indian," I said, nudging him roughly. "Something's in the yard." I didn't wait for him to answer, but jumped from bed and quickly dressed. I grabbed the Indian's old revolver from his sock drawer and a handful of bullets. He was still fumbling for his boardshorts when I made my way downstairs.

Inside the kitchen, the glowing electronics and metal appliances made everything seem like an underwater world. Our windows were open attempting to catch a breeze, and I paused to listen. A soft grumbling could be heard coming from the roosters' yard. I opened the kitchen door and snuck outside. Beneath my bare feet, the dirt was thick and moist. I started jogging toward the cages. The back gate was askew, and the cage doors were pushed aside. The teepees had been overturned in the yard, and Kū was bloodied and squawking near the side fence. In the back of the yard, a pack of three pit bulls were attacking something, and I knew without looking what it was. I screamed and waved my arms at the dogs, but they kept tearing at their prey. My hands were shaking. Still, I managed to load the gun, and then I did as the Indian had taught me that winter: I raised my arms straight in front of my chest and squared my stance. I pulled back the hammer. I took a deep breath, and I aimed.

The shot was lost in the darkness, but the sound startled the dogs and they looked up from the bundle of feathers in front of them. I pulled back the hammer again and fired, this time hitting one of the dogs in the side. The other two scattered like flies. I shot a third time into the space they had vacated, but the one dog was already down and the other two were running for the back gate. They tore up the hill to the road and disappeared. They were well-trained fighters. I didn't shoot again.

I walked up to the injured dog. Hapa lay beside the pit, dead, his feathers scattered across the yard and glued to the pit's mouth in a red, sticky mess. The dog was crying and growling at once. The bullet had gone into its chest, and though it tried to crawl away from me, it wasn't strong enough to stand and run. I stood over it helplessly. I was crying, I realized, and shaking, and I felt sorry for the dog and its mission.

No matter what the dog's owner had asked of it, however, I was the one who had shot it. I felt terrible, sorry for the animal and sorry for me. The dog gnashed its teeth at me and let out a long, lonely cry of pain. Its blood was pooling in the dirt. The Indian came up behind me. He reached for my right hand, which still held the gun, and took it from me. With the expertise of a trained hunter, he pulled back the hammer, aimed at the pit's head, and fired. The dog went limp. At last the night was silent again.

The Indian rested the gun on Hapa's cage. Keoni was still in his coop, but he was mad and pecking and I had a hard time locking him in without getting scratched. Kū had a crushed wing, probably injured when one of the teepees fell over. Lono had run toward the hen house. He calmed when I spoke to him and allowed me to carry him back to the yard. Of all of us, Lono seemed the least disturbed by the night's events.

While I washed Kū and bandaged his wing, the Indian righted the teepees and raked the yard clean. I placed Hapa gently into a trashbag, along with his feathers, and the Indian promised to drive the bag down to the city dump in the morning. We double-bagged the dead dog. He would go to the dump, too.

I checked on the hen house, and the chickens were unharmed. The Indian found a new set of locks and secured the back and front gates to the roosters' yard. The others had been cut and tossed on the ground.

Inside the house, I showered and let the hot water run on me for a long time. When I emerged from the bathroom, the Indian was waiting with a cup of tea. "Who do you think did this?"

"I don't know."

"Would they have come after you or me?"

"Whoever it was was jus' after the birds. That's why they sent dogs."

The Indian watched me, and for once I answered with the same silence he usually reserved for me. "What about your dad. I told you I hear things. People say he threw fights."

"What people? Jus' the jealous kind."

"They say he would switch bands so birds were fighting in lower weight classes. He would switch the birds, too."

"What a lie! If true, my uncle like tell me. If not, if he neva know,—"

"I'm sure your uncle did know. All those men probably do."

"My dad neva like dat," I yelled. "He da best pitta on island!"

" 'The,' not 'da,' " the Indian said automatically. "I've told you before I don't trust those men. And I don't like who you are with those birds."

"Maybe you don't like me an-y-more."

"I've never said that. I love you. You know that. But tonight, they could have hurt us. They could have hurt you." The Indian didn't sound angry.

I took a deep breath and placed my empty mug in the sink. "Tonight is never going to happen again." I looked into the Indian's eyes and placed a hand on his hip.

"So you'll stop fighting?"

I hesitated but then nodded.

"Promise?"

"Promise."

The Indian kissed me on the cheek, like he believed me, but when I went upstairs to bed, he didn't follow. I thought about what I had promised him, and I told myself I wasn't lying. I would stop, as soon as I beat Mr. Oh.

A couple hours later I awoke. The Indian's side of the bed was cool. When I looked out the window, his truck was gone, as were the bags of dead animal, and the roosters were already crowing that it was time to rise.

The Indian and I found our way back to a delicate re-creation of the past, the good months. He eventually returned to our bed, though this time without a poem tacked to the bathroom mirror, and when he wanted me, he took me in the dark, without whispering "Poi Dog," without watching me undress.

The September derby required a minimum of four birds, so I borrowed a black from Uncle Lee. When the

Indian asked why I had acquired a new bird, I told him I was just training the animal for my uncle. The Indian's eyes got small and dark, but he didn't say anything more.

I could have won back the Indian in the months that followed. I could have given up on the fighting, or given up preparing to fight. I could have given up on my dad, too, who I knew was dead and not coming back. I could have gone to the Indian and asked his forgiveness and felt him pull my body beneath his, the heat of his flesh warming mine, until I belonged to him completely. I had an entire summer to give the birds to Uncle Lee and rake clean the yard and dismantle the teepees and hear silence at dawn instead of the cocks crowing. Four months. But it could have been four years, or forty. I was the kind of girl who took care of things, who could be trusted. I couldn't go back on that now.

When September came I was ready. On the day of the fight, my uncle arrived with his truck. It had a covered bed, the kind that's perfect for hiding your birds from other competitors. We tucked the four cages beneath the tonneau cover, and I added containers of food and water. After my uncle left, I made a big show of cleaning up the yard, as if the birds were gone for good, and then I came back inside the house. The Indian was on the living room couch with a book of Bashō's poetry in his lap. He had a poker game later that evening, so I knew he would leave for town soon.

I clunked around in the kitchen for a while, pouring

myself water and mopping up spilled salad dressing, but the Indian didn't say anything. Finally, I couldn't stand the silence anymore. "I like think you're happy." I leaned on the couch's armrest, still dressed in my jeans and work shirt, reeking of bird shit and sweat.

"About what?" He had a bag of barbecue chips on the couch next to him, and he crunched on the chips without looking up from his book.

"I just gave my birds to Uncle Lee."

"Oh?"

"I gave them away. All pau."

The Indian closed his book. He looked up at me, his eyes clear and black as obsidian. "Done for good?"

"Yeah."

"Thank you." He rested his hand on mine. "You've given me the one thing I wanted most. I don't know what I'd do if you went back."

"Why go back?" I smiled, but I felt queasy.

"I'm going into town tonight. I have my poker game."

"Really? I was thinking that was next week."

I waited until the Indian left for town before driving to Uncle Lee's. Al was hosting, and Uncle Lee had promised to announce this fight rather than participate in it. Uncle Lee drove us to Al's along the back way, on a dirt road that wound for almost a mile through a dense forest of eucalyptus and New Caledonia pines before opening into a broad clearing. Al's house was a well-kept, one-story bungalow with checked blue-and-white curtains in the windows that spoke of a woman's presence. I wondered if Al's wife would be working with him. The smaller fights were usually all men, but the larger ones, like this one, drew out wives and girlfriends and even children. It was rare to see another woman by herself, but when one assisted with the weighing and banding, I was always glad. I felt calmer, and my birds seemed more relaxed as well.

The pit was set up behind the house beneath a large canopy the size of a basketball court. Stadium seating had been built with concrete blocks and wooden boards, and most of the pitters were already gathered near the pit, having their birds weighed and banded by Al and his nephew. I didn't see Mr. Oh, but I noticed that the pitters banded in front of Al now.

Uncle Lee parked his truck next to the podium, where he'd be making his announcements. The other men took turns keeping an eye on each other's roosters, or they kept the birds in cages under their seats. I kept my birds in the truck, where my uncle could watch them. I counted some two hundred entries on the matching board, meaning at least fifty pitters had come. The tent was crowded and misty with cigarette smoke, and I couldn't see much of anything in the blue haze hanging beneath the tent's eaves and along the top row of risers.

At around midnight Lono fought a runner, and we won easily. I had laid a sizable bet, so I collected nearly three hundred dollars. An hour later the black I had borrowed from my uncle fought. He took the first ten-second count but got hung on the second ten, and my opponent, Hao, a man I had lost to the year before, had to pull the spur from his bird's wing. Hao was short with a dark complexion and acne scars running like train tracks across his forehead. When he pulled the spur from his bird, he squeezed my black's leg and the bird pecked at the air.

"Watch it!" I said.

Hao glared at me. I glanced up at Al, but he shrugged as if he hadn't noticed, and I didn't want to make a fuss. My black would win this fight, I felt sure. I heard Al say, "Get ready!" I held my black at the score and put my left hand on my hip. My opponent did the same. "Pit!"

I released my black and he went at the other bird, pecking at its face and neck. The other bird didn't run, but it didn't fight back either, just dodged like a boxer. My bird took the second ten count. The last ten count went much the same, but in the twenty-count my black hung himself on his leathers. He wasn't bleeding, just confused, and he went back on the mat with a vengeance. The other bird looked tired. His wing was bleeding, but he was a tough rooster and didn't run. Still, the count went to my black and we won the match. Again, I collected.

I carried my black to Uncle Lee's truck and untied the gaff. I wanted to get him some water and a tablespoon of cornmeal with milk, but I needed to hold him first, calm him, thank him. I tucked him under my arm, humming slightly, and he went still. This was the praise he had been waiting for. I looked at the mat, where a couple of battle-cocks were pecking at each other, and then glanced into the stands. Men with cash in their hands were cheering on their birds. Other men were walking around outside, strolling to the porta-potties and back, or just taking a smoke break. To my left, I could see lights twinkling behind the windows of Al's bungalow.

"Good fight, girl." Al was behind me, his lopsided smile long and sweet. His nephew was judging this round.

"Thanks, Uncle."

"You ready fo' go up 'gainst Mr. Oh?"

"As ready as I eva be."

Al reached out and gave me a hug. When he pulled away, he looked at me for a long time, until I became embarrassed and stepped from him toward the truck. "I tell you someting, girl. Mr. Oh, he run an honest fight, but dese days I give anyting fo' have yoa papa back." Al kissed me softly on the cheek, as my father had once done. "I miss him. He was one good friend, no matta what."

I watched Al make his way back to the pit. He paused to shake hands with a couple of men, another he clapped on the back. The way those pitters watched him, I could see they respected him. They trusted him. Men didn't used to look at Al like that. They had never looked at my father like that.

I thought back to what the Indian had said about my father, and I wondered if I had been told the truth. Had my dad really been throwing fights? Switching bands? And had my uncle known this all along?

I felt confused, unsure of what I knew and didn't, of what was right and what wasn't. I wanted the Indian with me to tell me what to do, what to listen to. I longed to finger his short, wiry hair, to stroke his earlobes, soft as a chick's down and dotted with the old puncture marks of piercings. I wanted to hear him say "Poi Dog." I wanted to hear him say "Wanle." I wanted him to associate me with the dissipation of fear.

I looked around the tent for guidance or a sign, but all I saw was Mr. Oh on the opposite side of the pit holding his bird while his gaffer tied the knife. The other men watched Mr. Oh with awe and respect. I felt his power, and I wanted to take him down, for my father and my uncles. For me. What did it matter if my dad had been throwing fights? I asked myself.

I placed the black in his cage and brought out Keoni. He was restless, wriggling in my arms. I had to cover his eyes with my hands and sing to him before he'd calm down. Zoo wandered over to talk story. "Eh, Uncle," I said, kissing him on the cheek.

"Can help." He held his hands out to hold Keoni so I could tie the gaff. As I wound the leathers and checked the knife for its proper placement, Zoo chatted away, giddy with anticipation. Apparently, word had gone out that Mr. Oh and I were up next, and even the men who hadn't previously known the significance of the fight knew now.

Zoo watched me tie off the leather and grinned broadly. "Jus' like da dad, you. Mo betta even."

"My dad, was he really da best?"

"Ah, babe. He one of dem."

"You said he wen get help. What you mean?"

"Help is help. No mean yoa dad neva a great pitta, but. Jus', you know, da dad and Al and all us, we go way back, since we kids togeda. Da dad like win, and Al, he like host. We all like when he stay host. Or we did befoa Mr. Oh."

Zoo handed back Keoni. He brushed his fingers through the bird's hackle gently, fondly. "You folks helping me?" I asked.

"No. Yoa uncle said dis one yoa way." Zoo wrapped his arms around me, and Keoni pecked at the air. "Now go win 'em fo' Uncle Zoo. Get plenny money on dis fight!"

I watched Zoo shuffle back into the stands, and I understood: My dad hadn't been the greatest pitter after all, just a very good cheater. The Indian had been right. Uncle Lee and Zoo and Al all knew, were all part of my father's indiscretions. But Mr. Oh had talked, and my dad had been killed. No matter what he had done in the past, his honor still rested with me.

I looked up into the tent again and found the Indian on every riser. I shook my head and took my place on the edge of the pit. Mr. Oh stood not five feet away in a pair of crisp brown slacks and a blue polo shirt. He looked out of place, a country club man lost in the country. When I glanced in his direction, he gave me a curt nod.

We carried our birds to the mat and held them above the center score. His rooster was already cawing and scratching for the ground. Keoni seemed to have retreated into a deep meditation. When Al said, "Get ready," we both put our left hands on our hips. "Pit!" We dropped our birds.

Mr. Oh's black went for mine fast, and Keoni started to run. But at the second score he turned and held his ground with a couple of well-placed pecks to the face. Mr. Oh's bird responded in kind, and the first count went to them. Al called twenty seconds of rest, and then Mr. Oh and I lined up our birds at the second score. Keoni was more aggressive this time, pecking and using his gaff, and we took the second count. In the third ten, Mr. Oh's bird got his gaff into Keoni's breast feathers and was hung. I removed the knife and checked for a puncture wound. Blood had pooled beneath the feathers, but once I wiped down my boy with a damp washcloth, I could see the cut wasn't deep, just long.

I lined up Keoni at the third score, and at the call of "pit," Mr. Oh's bird went at my boy again. Keoni sustained cuts to his left wing and thigh. Mr. Oh's black took the count.

In the final rest I held Keoni under my arm and hummed. He was upset, in pain, snapping his beak in the air. I had only twenty seconds to calm him, to remind him I was there, waiting for him after he completed the fight. I smoothed his comb and patted his hackle. I cooed to him, then tugged gently at the gaff, testing its tightness, reminding him where it was. I walked to the center score, and at the call, dropped him on the mat.

For the first eight seconds the birds pecked at each other's faces. Keoni took a bad one to his right eye. Mr. Oh's bird had a deep cut beside his beak. Both birds raised their knives but neither could get a good hold on the other, and they mostly stabbed the air. At twelve seconds, Keoni managed to get his gaff into his opponent's breast, and he was hung. Mr. Oh's bird lifted its wings and tried to back away, but Keoni was stuck to him, tied by a knife and a will to win. Mr. Oh held his bird while I removed the gaff, and only then did I see how long and deep the gash was. Keoni had lunged the other bird. Mr. Oh righted his black on the mat and we let them go, but his bird was dizzy, blood filling the lung where my boy had stabbed. Keoni went at the other bird's face, pecking at its eyes and cheeks, and by the time the fight was called, Mr. Oh's black was on the ground, huffing, his eyes already turning misty and blue. Keoni continued pecking, relentless.

I lifted my boy off the other, who was trembling and shaking. Mr. Oh didn't even bother to look down. He held out his hand to shake mine. "You are not your father's daughter," he said in careful English. He paused before adding, "I will be honored to meet you again." Finally, he bent down and picked up the body of his bird. Then, on the mat where everyone could see, he gave his bird the screw. Its body went limp, and Mr. Oh walked off with the dead animal in his hands.

All around me I could hear men yelling and laughing and cursing. Some had won big, some had lost big, some just wanted me to leave the mat so the next match could start. As I walked off men clapped me on the back.

Zoo was waiting to hug me and give me a big, wet kiss on the cheek. Uncle Lee called me his baby girl and embraced me. They both told me the amounts of their bets, how much they had won, but I didn't hear them. I couldn't even feel the weight of their hands on my shoulders.

For Mr. Oh, what had this fight been? Just one among many? He had lost a bird, maybe a few hundred dollars, nothing more. He hadn't lost a father. And I hadn't regained one.

After I washed and taped Keoni's wounds, I secured his left wing so he wouldn't flap it. I caged him and secured the others, leaving them in my uncle's truck. I walked down the long driveway to the highway, and then toward my uncle's house. I wanted to go home. I was done.

I picked up my car at Uncle Lee's and drove fast down Haleakalā Highway, taking the curves with urgency. When I arrived home, the lights were off, the windows black. I parked and climbed out of the car, exhausted in every way. The Indian's truck wasn't parked in the driveway so I figured he was still in town with his buddies.

I dug in my purse for my keys, and when I found them, I pushed the diamond-shaped one into the keyhole. The key didn't fit. I tried my other two keys, and neither of them fit either. Confused, I walked around to the back of the house and tried my keys there, but again none of them opened the door. I looked around, suddenly unsure if in my weariness I had driven to the wrong house, but this was it. I was home. I didn't understand why my keys weren't working. I looked up at the windows and then behind me, at the cock yard, and that's when I saw what he had done.

The Indian had stuffed all my belongings into the roosters' coops. My clothes poked out between the wooden slats like errant feathers; photographs of my father and my uncle and me were piled in the feeding dishes; incense from my grandmother and a Carhartt jacket from Uncle Lee lay on a teepee; and my ledgers, all of them, where I had tracked my birds' diet and exercise regimes, their weight and moods, were stacked outside the nearest coop.

I started to put together what must have happened: The Indian had heard in town that a fight was on and he had returned home and seen me gone and known I had lied to him. Or he had known all along. Maybe he had even come to the fight, for a minute, to confirm his suspicions. Maybe I had actually seen him in the stands.

I walked around the yard, some small part of me impressed with his righteous anger. I would have to beg for forgiveness, I realized, and the opportunity to laugh this all away. I had, just an hour ago, truly given up the birds. I was finally done with the fighting, the men, the violence—all the things the Indian detested. If I asked him, he would take me back.

I spotted a turquoise negligee ballooning up from the back cage, and I laughed to think of the Indian stuffing all my underwear into a rooster coop. I would admit that his revenge was perfect, and I deserved it. I knew he would eventually forgive me, make keys to match the new locks, wash the smell of rooster shit off my clothes.

I was still smiling when I spotted a white, downy roll beneath the final coop. It looked like an old sweater of mine, and I bent down to pick the thing up. Only when my hand grazed its side did I feel the feathers and the remnants of body heat coming off the dead chick.

I ran to the hen house. The wire door was ajar, its wooden base bent and misshapen as if it had been kicked in. Hens lay strewn across the yard, and bullet casings littered the ground, the red plastic blending with the blood. Everywhere I saw feathers. White, ochre, orange, the peculiar blue-gray color down turns when wet: the feathers carpeted the ground. Black feathers melted into the shadows. Brown feathers blended with the dirt. Some of the hens looked like they were nesting, their feet tucked beneath their heavy breasts, while others had their wings spread, as if in flight, silhouetted against a muddy sky. I picked my way to the coop, careful not to step on any outflung wings. Several had fallen on their backs, legs sticking in the air like two flags of surrender, and these I took the time to turn over, on their sides, in a show of respect.

In the coop, every egg had been smashed. The wooden walls were yellow and glossy with yolk. I backed out slowly. I didn't want to touch anything in the coop, didn't even turn the rest of the birds on their side. I felt filthy. I felt dead myself.

I didn't bother to retrieve any of my clothes or belongings. I just climbed into my car and drove away.

I've had six years now to think about vengeance and forgiveness, to ponder my nature and those of the men I've known. These days I live in Honolulu, where I run little risk of seeing family or old acquaintances from Maui.

Three years ago I earned my Culinary Arts degree at Kapi'olani Community, and I now work downtown as a chef in an upscale French bistro. In my spare time, I write. At college I found an affection for the rigorous academic English the Indian had once imposed on me. Now pidgin is a translation of sorts, the speech of my past.

In my last semester at college I took a course in poetry and read the writers who once influenced him: Bashō, Issa, Buson. They write about the beauty and majesty of nature, and I understand why he loved them. But the Indian failed to understand their work in its fullness, how their poems at times celebrate the violence, loss, sadness, and cruelty inherent in the natural world.

When I left the Indian, I ran to the only person I knew who wouldn't ask why I was without my birds. My grandmother paid for a one-way plane ticket to O'ahu, and she helped me start my life here. In the months after I fled

Maui, rumors spread that I had come to O'ahu seeking Mr. Oh's bosses, the men who had arranged for my father's death. Some claimed I murdered my hens because my win had meant so little to Mr. Oh. Others said I left the Indian because he had refused to help me kill Mr. Oh. I ignored everything. It belonged to another era, another life.

In the intervening years, my grandmother and I have found our way into the sort of relationship I suspect she had hoped for after my father's death. In our phone conversations, I describe the restaurant's patrons, the meals I create, the friends I've made. She gives me the news from Maui. Zoo died of a heart attack last spring, but Uncle Lee and Al are still around, fighting birds and taking bets as they've always done. They ask after me, but my grandmother tells them little.

The Indian still lives in Makawao, alone. He keeps the rooster coops just as they were when I was still living there. He is not the same man he was, Uncle Lee tells my grandmother. My uncle thinks my leaving broke him, but I know this isn't true. The moment the Indian killed that first bird, he returned to his childhood home, his father's child.

For a long time I missed him. I ached for him. I wanted to send him the essays I wrote in school or the menus I created for the restaurant or a picture of those boulders in Makawao bathed in the last light of the day. I wanted him to know I'd become the woman he wanted.

I dreamt of him as I once dreamt of my father. In every storefront shadow I saw the outline of his broad shoulders. In every dark bed I wondered if he was waiting for me. At times I was tempted to write to the Indian, but my grandmother always talked sense into me. In other moments I wished I could just write about the Indian, about my father, about my uncles and those birds. I wanted to commit them to paper and then leave them there.

That I have finally succeeded in speaking of those men—the most important in my life and the most disappointing—is, oddly enough, thanks to Mr. Oh. Not long ago, after closing up the kitchen at the bistro, I walked to the Blue Conch for a pau hana before returning home. I took a corner stool in the back where I wasn't likely to be interrupted and ordered a beer. Diagonally across from me sat a man I almost didn't recognize. He looked old and tired. His polo shirt was speckled with food stains, smudges browned his collar. A long scar ran from beneath his left ear to just under his chin. From the way he held himself, stiff and regal, though wary now, too, I knew it was Mr. Oh.

When I gave him the same curt nod he had afforded me at that derby so long ago, his eyes grew, and he scooted from the bar. I guessed that he, too, had heard the rumor I was seeking out his bosses, and he must have thought I had also come for him.

I followed him outside. "Wait," I called from the bar entrance.

He was across the street and several storefronts down, but he paused. He looked over his shoulder and in that same careful English said, "It is over for me now. You know that, do you not?"

I wanted to assure him I meant no harm and the islands' gossips were not to be trusted, but he didn't wait to hear me. He hurried down the street and disappeared into an alley. For a moment I was frustrated by his departure, by his refusal to listen to me, but then I felt a great release. I can only describe it as the relief of loss. I now haunted him as once he had haunted me. This was my revenge: I had liberated myself from those men, but they could not be free of me.

As I looked down the empty street, the shadows hid nothing. I didn't hope to see the silhouette of the Indian. I didn't hope to return to the life I once had. *Wanle,* I said to myself. *It is done. They are all gone.*

THE ROAD TO HĀNA

He'd be happy with Becky forever, Cameron thought on their flight to Maui, and again when they rented the little Chevy Aveo, and even when they'd stopped for a late breakfast in Pā'ia and she poured shoyu on her fried eggs and the liquid left black streaks through the yolks. She had told him that she wanted to buy a condo in Honolulu, but now he wondered aloud if eventually she'd wish to return to Vegas because her parents and aunts and uncles were there.

"Never," she said, reaching for his hand across the glass tabletop. They were sitting on the restaurant's patio, close to the kitchen, and through the screen door he could hear the cooks' laughter and the sizzle of the grill. "I came back here to stay."

Cameron squeezed her hand in his. "But you should feel free to change your mind. Go where the jobs are or where the adventure lies."

"You can be so silly sometimes!" she laughed. She stood and walked around the café table, then sat herself in his lap. Her fingers were cool against his temple. A stray dog wandered onto the open patio and sniffed along the bottom of the kitchen door. Cameron tossed it a slice of toast. "If you leave, I'll go with you," he promised.

Becky didn't answer him right away, but later, in the car, she said, "It's just you and your parents here, but for me there's an entire ancestry. I'm not going anywhere, Cam. This is my real home."

Cameron appreciated her reassurance. He loved her for it. And yet, he wondered what Honolulu was if not *his* real home. He had been born there, raised there. His parents and friends were there. He taught history at McKinley High, and his students respected him. Just because his parents were born in Minnesota didn't mean Hawai'i wasn't his.

She held out a bottle of sparkling water. "Because you're always dehydrated after a big breakfast," she said, and kissed his cheek. He smiled then because she was right and she knew him so well. He took a long sip from the bottle, and as they drove out of Pā'ia he turned the radio to her favorite Hawaiian music station. Houses gave way to cane fields, which ascended Haleakalā's gentle slope. Dense clouds hid the crater's upper reaches. All the plants were green, even the scrub beside the road, and it was hard to imagine he was ever thirsty here.

Just before Māliko Bay the radio went to white noise.

Cameron ignored it. He needed to concentrate on the road, the way the Hāna Highway followed the topography of the cliffs, teetering above the ocean, then turning tightly inland.

"See that church?" Becky pointed to a whitewashed chapel. "My auntie was married there. My grandma's sister." The church was small, trimmed in a rust-red reminiscent of the color of volcanic soil.

"It's so quaint."

"Isn't it?" She squeezed his knee with her hand. "Her holokū was all lace, and she made every inch of it herself. Can you imagine?"

"Is that one of the traditional skills you want to learn? Sewing your own wedding dress?"

"Hardly," she giggled. "I'll learn to pound kapa, but lace-making I'm happy to leave in the past."

"It's from the missionaries anyways," he teased her.

"Exactly." Her tone was serious. "My aunt's dress was beautiful, though. I'll show you the pictures one day."

The car coasted down a hill and settled into a curve that reminded him of the inside of Becky's elbow, the smooth pocket of her *antecubital fossa*. Becky was in her second year of residency at Queen's Medical Center in Honolulu, and she was teaching him the scientific terms for his body. Sometimes he'd pick her up at the end of her shift and she'd tell him what she'd treated that day: scapular fracture, septicimia, tarsal dislocation. He enjoyed the sound of these words, like coral popping underwater. He loved watching her mouth moving around the syllables, her tongue tapping against her palate and her teeth flashing white beneath her chapped lips. From her even "influenza" sounded urgent and exotic.

She gestured toward a bamboo forest at the side of the road where the reeds grew densely together. He had once been to a bamboo forest in Japan, outside of Kyoto, where he studied for a year in college. Paths had been cut through the forest, and the bamboo grew in thick arches that curved over the walkways. The light that managed to trickle through the leaves was thin and green. A girl had taken him there. His girlfriend at the time. He could still see the way her black hair hung straight and thick, its blunt cut running parallel to her bra strap, the outline of which he glimpsed beneath her white blouse. She had run ahead, and when she turned to tell him something, the viridian light caught in her hair and turned it a deep turquoise.

"One of my uncles used to dig up the bamboo shoots," Becky said. "He'd boil them all day, until they were soft, and then cook with them." She rested her head on his shoulder, and he could smell the piney scent of her shampoo. "I wish everyone was still here."

"Me, too. I'd ask your uncle to cook for me!"

She laughed. "He'd love that. He loves feeding people."

"Were you happy when the rest of the family moved to Vegas? You were all together then."

"We were, but then it wasn't the same. Everyone was far from home."

"Were they happy when you left for O'ahu?"

"I guess. They didn't really say." She tucked her legs underneath her and offered Cameron her hand.

"Maybe they were jealous. Not angry jealous, just sort of wistful."

"Maybe. It's funny, they spent years trying to get my parents to move back here, and now they're always asking me when I'm coming home to Vegas. But I tell them, Vegas isn't home. It's not where I'm from."

"But you were born there. That doesn't make you less Hawaiian, but it does make you something else, in addition. Maybe Vegasian." He waited for her to laugh, but she was quiet, thinking about something.

"I know it's hard growing up haole on the islands. You've said before the teasing was rough." She paused. "I never got teased for being Hawaiian. No matter where you are, being Hawaiian is cool. But in some ways, I think it was harder growing up Hawaiian and *not* being here. That sense of displacement, of never quite fitting in."

He brushed his fingers through her hair, and she held his hand there, his palm warming the corner of her earlobe. "I know that feeling. I used to think, I wouldn't stick out if my parents went back, if we were in our homeland."

"Germany?"

"Minnesota."

"I think the Ojibwa might take issue with you calling Minnesota your homeland." Now she laughed, as if she were teasing him.

"But I'm not from Germany. My parents and grand-parents weren't from Germany. They're Minnesotans through and through."

She sighed and lifted her hand from his. He let his fall back to the steering wheel. "My cousin can chant back twenty-five generations. That's what it means to be from a place. And yet, you're from Minnesota, and I'm from Vegas. How can that be?"

He wanted to say he wasn't from Minnesota. He was from Hawai'i. Yet, that didn't seem quite right. He was local, he knew that much. He was local and she wasn't. But did that matter? Was local being from a place, or just of it? "I have to think about what you said."

"I like when you think." She took his hand again. "I'm happy we're doing this. It's good to take a vacation together."

She looked out the window then, her cheek pressed against the plastic wall of the car, her hair tangling in the wind. They passed a house with two tireless cars in the yard and a lime green schoolbus on blocks. A dog lay panting beneath it in the cool dirt. "Remember when we went to North Shore together for the first time?" she said. "You packed your truck with a cooler of food and that tiny bridge on the way to Waimea was covered in water. The waves were practically at the road, and you wanted to keep the windows rolled up with the air-conditioning on, and I wouldn't let you. It's like that every time, isn't it?"

"I get hot is all."

"And I don't like the smell of air through the conditioner. It's too clean."

"What's wrong with clean air?"

"It doesn't smell like Hawai'i. It's just like after you shower and all I smell is that green soap you use. You don't smell like you."

"What does me smell like?" He winked at her in the reflection of the windshield.

"Like mushrooms and dried limu and raw beef about to go bad."

He made a face. "Sounds disgusting."

"No, it's wonderful." She brought her mouth to his ear and whispered: "You smell like a man."

Happiness was a balloon inflating inside his chest. He felt for the backpack behind his seat: inside its left pocket, tucked underneath a battery charger, was the ring. He ran his fingers along the nylon shoulder strap. The dozens of ridges in its weave were smooth and slippery.

"Tell me something else," he said.

"Something else." She smiled. "How about this: I love you like a wave loves sand."

He thought of how the ocean unfurls in every direction on the beach and then retracts like a gigantic, curling tongue. "Hungrily?"

"Powerfully."

The road crested and Cameron glimpsed a narrow inlet. The cliff walls were sheer, black rock, and the road hugged them, falling steeply. As they descended toward sea level, Mustang convertibles lined the narrow road, parked in even narrower turnouts. Every convertible had its top down. Between hala trees he glimpsed a couple of twentysomething girls walking gingerly across the stone beach. They held hands, fingers knitted together, arms raised above their heads as they tried to balance against one another. He saw a flash of hot pink, a purple flower pattern, a bare stomach. A little boy was collecting stones near the side of the road and placing them carefully in a red sand bucket.

"Tourists," he said.

"They remind me of crabs. The color of their skin."

Cameron nodded in agreement, then realized he didn't feel the same. He knew tourists by their choice of car, not their skin color. Locals didn't drive convertibles; they drove trucks. With air-conditioning.

They reached the bottom of one hill and began to ascend another. To their right, a narrow ravine cut deeply into the mountainside. The rock was hidden by the flat, feathered leaves of palapalai ferns, and two hundred feet above a waterfall surged over the cliff edge. The falls were white and slender, like the waist of a young girl. On the ground, the water streamed through the ravine and then beneath a narrow bridge, before being deposited into the ocean. Cameron pulled to the side of the road to let two cars headed in the opposite direction pass over the bridge first.

"You had the right of way," Becky said.

"But they're coming downhill. It's safer to let them go."

She shrugged and looked out the window.

He felt her drifting from him and struggled to find a way to draw her back. "So why is Hāna so important to the Hawaiian people?" he asked finally. They were high on a cliff again, above the harsh winds that made the water take on the wrinkled appearance of elephant skin. The sky was the same color as the sea, and only its smooth surface separated it from the ocean.

"In ancient days, Hāna is a vacation spot for the Big Island chiefs," Becky said. She always spoke of history in the present tense, which never failed to unsettle him. To him, history was not available for reintroductions and re-living but accessible only via careful and protracted study. For Becky, however, the past and present existed in the same moment. In her memory the two met, and through their meeting, she layered them, until the past and present were like ocean and sky, without noticeable boundary. "The chiefs paddle the channel between Big Island and East Maui, spending their summers in Hāna. They build second homes even. So when King Kamehameha and his armies want to conquer Maui, they land in Hāna first because they know the people won't rise up against them. They will be torn between allegiances."

"And are they?" He corrected himself: "*Were* they?"

"I guess. They tell the Maui chiefs that Kamehameha has landed, but they don't fight him. I suppose they can't. They are outnumbered. They don't want to fight. East Maui has never been known for its warriors."

"How do you know that?"

"Know what?"

"That East Maui isn't known for its warriors."

Her eyes lifted to the upper right corner of their sockets until he saw the fine, red veins at the outer corner. Finally, she said, "I suppose I read it somewhere. Wherever I read about the battle. Why do you ask?"

"It just seems like an odd blanket statement. An entire portion of an island not being known for its ability to fight? That's an era when everybody would have been trained to fight."

She threw up her hands and let them land with a smack on her bare thighs. He noticed how her skirt had edged up her legs, her skin smooth and brown, and he almost regretted challenging her. "This is how Hāna folks are known today. As farmers, not fighters."

"But what of then?"

"What of then?" She turned her head toward him. He looked at her lips. They were lightly closed, not pressed together in anger, but closed all the same.

"What are you thinking?" he asked carefully.

She sighed. He could sense she wanted to tell him something but chose not to. Instead, she said, "I'm reminded of driving out here as a little girl. My dad is taking the curves too fast and my mom keeps saying she's dizzy. That's how they always are. You drive much slower."

"I have to go slow. I haven't driven this road as many times as your dad."

"I didn't mean it as a bad thing. I like how you drive. Cautiously, carefully." She leaned across the console and kissed him gently on the cheek. "You're a good man, Cam." He wanted to ask why she had said that, but he hesitated and then it was too late. "You know what?" she said, sitting up on her knees. "The trees are the same color now as when I was a child."

"Your memory is a vise," he laughed.

"I can't help it."

"I don't mind. I figure as long as I have you, I never have to remember anything on my own."

She raised her right eyebrow and touched her tongue to the bud of her upper lip. "Oh, I'll make sure you remember a few things." She reached her hand between his legs and curled her fingers around the crotch of his boardshorts. He tried to focus on the road even as her fingers thrummed gently against his testicles. She smiled up at him, her mouth slightly open, as if she was about to laugh or kiss him or both. He felt himself get hard. He wanted to watch her, the movement of her face, the creases squeezing at the corners of her eyes, her lower lip curving over her labiomental fold, that soft indentation above her chin.

She slid her thumb between the Velcro fastenings of

his shorts. He glanced away from the road again. Her hair hung over her eyes. She had worn it down just for him. Usually the soft curls framed her cheekbones, making her face appear lean and delicate, but today the humidity had weighed down her hair, and she looked different to him. She was breathing warmly on his thigh. He studied her for a moment longer. He wanted to remember her like this.

He looked up just in time.

The dog was in the middle of the lane. It had lifted its left foreleg and frozen, staring at Cameron. He slammed on the brakes. The tires screeched against the asphalt. He closed his eyes, waiting for the impact. A lumpy bump. He heard Becky's shoulder hit the dashboard, hard. She yelped. He opened his eyes. The dog hadn't moved. It watched him.

"I'm so sorry," he said, gasping. "Are you okay?" He didn't look at Becky, just kept his eyes on the dog, and he felt as if he was addressing the animal rather than her.

She followed his gaze out the windshield. Her hand was still on his leg, her weight now, too, but she didn't seem to notice how she was pressing against him. He saw her see the dog. The animal was black and white, with longish hair that had collected dirt and leaves. Cameron waited for it to run, dash into the forest to their right or scramble down the incline to their left. Becky lifted her hand from his leg. He wanted the dog to make a decision. *Go on,* Cameron thought to himself. *Make a move.*

He heard the passenger door open, and suddenly

Becky was on the two-lane road. A guy in a red convertible honked behind them, started to pull past, and then had to brake hard to avoid hitting her. "What in the hell?" the man yelled.

Becky didn't seem to hear him. Her attention was on the dog. She held out her arm, the back of her hand facing it in a practiced way. The dog eased toward her, sniffing her. Somewhere behind Cameron another car honked. He wanted to yell at them that his girlfriend was trying to save a dog. And he wanted to yell at Becky to get the hell in the car and leave the animal to its fate. He wanted all these things at once, and he didn't understand why Becky was scooping up the large dog in her arms.

Becky's legs peeped out from beneath the dog's body. Its lean face replaced Becky's head. She wrestled it toward the car, the dog squirming to be released, or perhaps with delight, for as soon as Becky loosened her grip it leapt into the front passenger seat and settled itself there. It had big eyes, deep brown and watery, and it looked up at Cameron with great expectation.

"No," Cameron said, looking at the dog. "Not in the front seat." The red convertible screeched past their Aveo. Two more cars followed. Cameron watched them with something akin to jealousy.

Becky lifted the mutt's hind legs and pushed it into the backseat. It sat in the center, leaning forward, its nose sticking between the two front seats. Becky pulled her door closed. "Ready?"

"For what? Where are we going?" Cameron turned to face her, but the dog was there, breathing on his shoulder. Long, curling lines of spit drooped from the dog's open mouth and onto Cameron's T-shirt. "Gross."

"He's lost. We have to find his house." Becky tickled the underside of the dog's neck and then pushed him back when he tried to step on the center console. "Stay!" she commanded. The dog sat.

Cameron put the car into drive again, though he didn't know where they were going. The dog had no collar. No collar meant no tags, and no tags meant no address. Still, Becky was insistent. "We'll just turn down the next road. These communities are so small. Someone will recognize him."

"It." Cameron pressed the gas pedal.

Becky frowned at him. "Look." She pointed to the dog's underside. "The dog's a 'he.'"

Cameron didn't reply. He watched for a turnoff, but they'd already passed the one for Ke'anae and, if he remembered correctly, Wailua was another five miles. There was no way the dog had traveled that far on the highway. "We have to turn around." Cameron lowered the windows all the way. The dog stank.

She nodded, serious. "You're right." She gripped his right arm, and her fingers dug into his skin. She leaned over to kiss him but the dog was there again, panting on Cameron's cheek, its breath smelling of rancid trash and shit, and Cameron turned his face away. She laughed.

"Back," she commanded, and again the dog retreated to the backseat.

Cameron found a turnout at the top of a cliff and pulled a U-turn. He headed back toward Ke'anae. In the rearview, Cameron watched as the dog circled twice and then plopped down on the backseat. It looked at him and panted, its lips stretched into a smile, and Cameron smiled back. He really wasn't so bad. Cameron just needed to recover from the shock of nearly hitting him and Becky's impulsive rescue. Cameron didn't like the way she had jumped into traffic, the cars honking at her. She had made him feel helpless. He chastised himself for not getting out with her or at least yelling at the jerk in the red convertible.

Becky rested her hand on his thigh again, and for a moment he could imagine them years from now, in a car like this one, their own dog in the backseat and a road in front of them, a vacation, a life. Yes, this was what he wanted: Becky, a dog, a baby or two, and an endless stretch of road. "I love you," he said. He wanted her to feel the weight of their future, too, the hope of it and the moment of it folding over on the present. She smiled softly and then peered back at the dog.

"Uh-oh," she whispered.

"What?" He slowed the car and glanced in the rearview. The dog's chest hair was delicate, white giving way to a pale tawny color. Beneath these fine tendrils, next to its pinkish skin, three thick, black lines of fleas were snaking through the fur. The fleas streamed beneath the stray's armpits and up into the dark scruff of its neck. They disappeared over the dog's sides, finding their way onto its back, and he pictured them hopping on to the upholstery in great parabolic leaps.

He hit the brakes in the middle of a hill. "Get it out of the car!" To their left was a rock cliff. To their right the incline fell precipitously toward the ocean several hundred feet below.

"We can't leave him here!" Becky squealed. "Just keep driving. We'll turn off at the first road."

Cameron hit the gas and the car jolted forward. The dog was thrown against the backseat. It yelped, and Becky glared at Cameron. She reached back to pet the animal, soothe it. "Don't touch it. You'll get fleas all over you!" he warned.

"Stop it!" She glared at him, her hands buried in the dog's fur. Cameron turned away, disgusted.

In two minutes he spotted a road that led in the direction of the ocean. He turned down it, relieved an exit had appeared so quickly. He didn't see any houses, and the asphalt soon gave way to gravel, but he continued at top speed. Becky and the dog bounced in their seats. "Slow down," she said, but he ignored her.

When the road evened out, they spotted a house. An iron gate surrounded the property, and a swimming pool glittered behind the entrance. "We can leave it here," he said.

"He doesn't belong here."

"How do you know?"

"It's obvious. A house like this? It's too nice for him. And anyway, we can't get him behind the gate. He'll run back to the highway again."

"Oh, sure, now the house is too good for it. Have you thought about if this dog is just a stray? Maybe it doesn't belong to anyone. Maybe we should have left it on the road."

"We'll take him down to the ocean then," she said. "We'll leave him by the water. At least he'll be far away from the highway, and maybe someone will adopt him."

"Do you think people here adopt stray dogs?"

She crossed her arms. "You are so negative. Just drive."

A half mile farther they spied a tan bungalow with white trim, a clean, simple house. No gate or fence surrounded it, just half-dead grass that needed to be cut. The house didn't look abandoned, but it had a lonely air.

Becky pointed to the driveway, and he followed it until they were only a few yards from the front porch. He threw the parking brake. "Get it out."

She opened her door and then the back one. "Come here, baby," she cooed, holding wide her arms as if expecting the dog to leap into them. But it didn't budge, only rested its head on its paws and looked at them with a forlorn expression.

"I'll push him from the other side." Cameron opened the back door and shouldered the dog toward Becky. "You pull."

"Pull what? I don't want him to bite me."

"Just a minute ago you were calling it 'baby.'"

She rolled her eyes at Cameron and then reached under the dog's front legs, tucking her hands beneath the animal's armpits. Cameron nudged the dog's butt toward Becky. The stray curled its forelegs over her shoulders, as if dancing, and its chest met hers. It looked over its shoulder at Cameron, a look that asked, Why is this happening, what have I done wrong to deserve punishment? and for a second Cameron felt sorry for the animal.

Despite its size, Becky carried it to the porch steps. She put it down and commanded it to stay, and the dog sat obediently. But when she started back toward the car, the animal sprinted past her and hopped into the backseat again. Cameron grunted in frustration, and the dog cowered. Cameron wished it had growled, shown some fight.

"This time, when you're holding him, I'll shut the doors."

As soon as Cameron had pushed the dog into Becky's arms again, he slammed the door on his side. Then he ran around to her side and closed the door there. She set the dog down on the yellow grass. Without waiting for a command, the dog ran to the driver's side of the car and jumped into the open window. It didn't make it all the way through, though, and was stuck, head and chest inside the car and hind paws scraping against the exterior. "Motherfucker!" Cameron yelled.

Becky pressed her lips together, but she didn't say anything. Cameron walked around to the window and lifted the dog's hind legs so it could clamber into the car. Then he opened the door and rolled up all the windows. The dog sat happily in the driver's seat, its head tilted in Cameron's direction, its ears perked.

"Try again," he said to Becky with forced calm.

"I know we can't keep him, but this just seems so . . ." Her voice trailed off.

"He's a poi dog, practically feral. He can handle himself." Cameron didn't mean to sound unfeeling, but he knew he did.

For the third time she lifted the dog into her arms, and it squirmed against her happily. She set it on the porch and ran back to the car. Cameron revved the engine. Gravel shot from the back tires.

"Slow down! The rocks will hit him!" Becky shrieked.

He slowed a little, but clouds of dust still blossomed behind them. The dog's barking could be heard through the windows. Cameron pressed the gas pedal again and the car gained speed, ascending the hill with ease, until the barking had faded and the dust was far in the distance and the tires gripped the asphalt, revolving with a smooth, even cadence. He looked over at Becky. Her shirt was covered in tiny black pinpricks. "Your shirt," he said, pointing. "Wipe it off!"

She acted as if she hadn't heard him. "Keep driving. I don't want the dog to follow us back to the highway where he could be hit." She sat perfectly still, her hands tucked beneath her thighs, the fleas flecking her skin. He slapped at his ankles. Her face was wet.

They drove in silence for a mile until Cameron found a lookout where he could pull off the highway. They both got out and tried to brush the fleas from their bodies and from the backseat with their hands. He hoped they were hopping out of the car and into the dirt. He couldn't bear if they were as stubborn as the stray.

"I'd like to take some pictures of the water," Becky said quietly. She seemed to have entered a world separate from Cameron's.

"Let's just get back on the road." The sun would soon dip behind Haleakalā, and he was anxious to get to the campsite while they still had daylight. He wanted to set up the tent and swim in the Seven Sacred Pools.

"We can take our time," she said. "I'll drive."

"We've lost too much time already. On account of the dog."

"We had to save him." Her voice was high and tight.

"You had to save it," he corrected.

She leaned into the car and pulled her camera from the front seat. "You're right. You would have been happy to let him be hit. It's amazing you stopped for him at all." She fiddled with the camera lens. After a moment, she looked up at him again. "I just don't understand how a man who can care so little for a dog can say he loves me."

Cameron let a hard laugh escape him. "Are you kidding? You are not a dog. You and the dog are two separate entities."

"I don't see things that way." Becky walked away from him and stood beside the edge of the lookout. Below her, the water was the color of sapphires.

He followed her to the edge of the cliff. "You're too sensitive about these things."

"Too sensitive?" She shook her head. "I'm not *too* anything. I'm just myself."

"But can't you be a little less of a bleeding heart? The dog would have been fine."

"You're cold," she said quietly. "I'm sensitive, and you're cold."

"That's not fair." He threw his hands up in exasperation.

"I don't know if this was a good idea."

"What does that mean?" He wanted to grip her shoulders and shake her, or pull her to him and hold her. Or both. Instead, he bent down and scratched his ankle.

"Maybe we shouldn't have taken this trip after all."

He rested his hands on her shoulders and looked into her eyes. He saw disappointment there. "I want to marry you," he said.

She ran her fingers through her hair and released a long, slow sigh. "Can you ask me again later?"

She retreated to the car, but he remained standing at the edge of the cliff looking over the water. The light had shifted while they were rescuing the dog, and now the sky was pale against the deep blue of the ocean and the horizon was a thin, white line.

They swam in the Seven Sacred Pools as the sun set. She pointed out that the pools were not sacred in ancient Hawaiian lore. He noted there were more than seven.

They did not speak of his proposal, and he wondered if he should try again, this time on one knee, with the ring in his hand. He would wait, he decided, until after they ate their dinner. He would wait until they were laughing again.

He caught six freshwater shrimp, which they boiled over their campfire after the sun had gone down. They peeled the shell from the shrimp tails and pulled the meat out with their fingers. She didn't like the heads, so she gave hers to him and he sucked on them. The shrimp were large, bigger than jumbo shrimp in a restaurant, and they had the clean, fresh taste of the river water.

"I would like them more if they tasted briny," she said. "Of the ocean."

"I like them like this."

She didn't answer. In the firelight her eyes were shadowed and her brows, thick and dark, appeared like marker lines on her face. He thought of the girl he had dated during his year in Japan and the way her brows had seemed so delicate and finely shaped on her oval face. Why hadn't he and that girl stayed together? What had come between them?

"I'm still hungry," Becky said. "Are you? I'll fix sandwiches."

"No, I'm full," he said, though he was still hungry, too. He had caught the shrimp and wanted to feel that he had provided enough for her.

She made two peanut-butter sandwiches with guava jelly and handed one to him. "I'm full," he repeated, but she left the sandwich on its paper towel beside him. She ate hers quickly, then washed her face and hands, using the washcloth to rub gently behind her ears. She could be fastidious when she wanted to be. While she brushed her teeth, he ate the sandwich and was glad he did. But he didn't thank her, just threw the paper towel into the fire and watched the white paper catch fire, flame, and then collapse into a million black particles.

He crawled into the tent beside her. "You smell like peanut butter," she giggled, kissing him.

She climbed on top of him and untied her bikini top. She wriggled out of her shorts, then reached beneath his shirt and tugged it over his head. He flipped her on her back and hovered above her, his chest touching her chest, his shorts rubbing against her bikini bottoms. He kissed her behind her ear where just moments before she had washed her skin. Her flesh had the green scent of fresh water, but her earlobe tasted of salt.

Outside the campfire was dying, and inside the tent

the light was dim. Still, the white of her breasts startled him. He had forgotten how pale they were compared to the rest of her body.

"I'll marry you," she said running her hand along the bumps of his spine.

She unfastened the Velcro of his shorts and tugged at the fabric until the shorts gathered at his knees. She slipped out of her bikini bottom. He was hard and wanted to be inside her. He bent down to kiss her stomach. Outside the firewood popped and a small flame blazed, filling the tent with a sudden orange light that faded as quickly as it had flared. A shadow flitted over her body, and Cameron thought suddenly of the fleas, their thick lines weaving across the dog's chest, and the way Becky had sat motionless when the bugs later landed on her. He felt his desire wither, and pushed himself away.

THIRTY-NINE RULES
FOR MAKING A HAWAIIAN FUNERAL
INTO A DRINKING GAME

1) Take a drink each time the haole pastor says "hell."

2) Take a drink each time he asks if anybody in the room wants to go there.

3) Take a drink each time he looks at one of your uncles when he says this.

4) Take a drink because cane was burning next to Kaumuali'i Highway on the drive from Kekaha to Poipu, and the hot scent reminded you of your grandmother's house with its upright piano, rattan furniture, and that deep cement sink in the washroom where laundry was scrubbed, and sometimes babies, too. In the family room you and your older cousins used to jostle each other, each of you hoping to be the one who got to sit on Grandma's lap in her high-backed butterfly chair.

One year ago you moved to Honolulu from Los Angeles, just to be closer to her, and now she's gone.

5) Drink when the pastor claims deeds get us into

heaven. Deeds like tithing to the church. Deeds like tithing to *his* church. (Do not comment on how this is unbiblical. Do not comment on how he encouraged your grandmother to give until she had no money left for the upkeep of her house. Do not comment on the Louis Vuitton man-purse you've seen him carry into church.)

6) Sneak a swig when the pastor asks everyone to hold hands and confess the sins in their hearts. Get stuck with his doughy palm in yours. Do not respond when he gives your fingers an encouraging squeeze. Do not interrupt when he prays for your family's wayward souls. Instead, look mournfully at the casket where your grandmother lies, and blame her for his presence.

7) After the sermon, approach the casket for the final viewing. Take a sip for each handmade paper lei and crayon drawing your little cousins have gently placed on top of your grandmother's hands. Do not touch her cheeks, which are full and in the dew of a freshly painted blush. Do not kiss her forehead as your cousins might, nor adjust the sleeve of her Sunday mu'umu'u, the one with the red hibiscus pattern, like your aunties do. You may, however, wrap a fine, gray-white tendril of hair around your finger and remember how you used to comb these same strands as she dozed in the hospital bed.

8) With your degree in English, your aunties expect you to deliver the most grammatically correct homage to your grandmother. Take this responsibility seriously. Your copyediting skills are all you have to offer your family.

After all, you were not born on Kaua'i. You weren't even born in Honolulu. No, you were raised a California girl, like your mother before you. She is haole. White. A foreigner. This makes you hapa haole. Half white. Half foreign.

Your eight-year-old cousin is dancing a hula. She hovers on the balls of her feet, her slender hips swaying like a palm. A neighbor's boy strums "Amazing Grace" on a child-size 'ukulele.

You cannot hula or play the uke. You do not speak pidgin. You never add the right proportion of water to poi. But you can summarize your grandmother's life in a five-paragraph essay, complete with thesis and topic sentences. And for this, you owe yourself a drink.

9) Approach the podium. Look out at your family tucked into neat rows. The mortuary has upholstered the pews in a warm beige color. The walls are sand-hued. You want to disappear into this uniformity. In your nervousness, forget to introduce yourself. During the eulogy, drink each time you say the words "family," "faith," or "the." Drink for every family member who gets teary during your speech. Drink for reading through the introduction and body paragraphs without taking a breath.

Conclude with a description of your grandmother seated at her kitchen table, the Bible in her hand, her illness not yet evident. Notice your dad wiping his eyes and realize you are seeing him cry for the first time in three years, since his favorite dog passed away. Lose your place in the speech. Forget, momentarily, your grandmother's name. Recall how squeezing her hand in yours felt like holding a fragile bird, and then feel your throat tighten, and tears threaten, and the steadiness of your voice wavering. Emma. Her name was Emma.

Feel angry that your family is making you deliver the eulogy. Rescind this. You are angry they are witnessing your grief. Drink.

10) Ask the family to share their memories of your grandmother. Rush back to your seat and search nervously for your father's hand. Hold it. Hold it as you did when you were eight—desperately, with need and fear. Down the rest of your beer.

11) During the hour of sharing, take a drink each time a family member avoids using the word "Alzheimer's."

12) An eighth cousin four times removed comes to the podium and expresses surprise at having just learned your grandmother was ill. Respond by sneaking a drink for each year your grandmother lived in the dementia wing of Hale Kūpuna (two), the years before that during which your auntie cared for her (three), and the year when the family first noticed your grandmother's memory slipping, her feet unsteady, her weight dropping because she could never remember to eat.

13) Take a drink when this eighth cousin four times removed promises that she, like your grandmother, has denied the sins of the flesh. She does not want to go to hell. She has been saved.

14) Take a drink each time she runs from the podium to the casket, drapes herself over your grandmother, and loudly sobs.

15) Take a drink when she has to be dragged away from the body.

16) Take a drink when both your uncle and dad ask, "Who dat?"

17) Sneak a sip when the cousin who fights MMA takes the podium. He describes how your grandma cared for him after he returned from Desert Storm with shrapnel in his knee, and how she made him attend church with her in hopes of giving him hope. Lean in when your cousin relates how, once, he brought his girlfriend to visit, and Grandma made him sleep in the living room. Late that night, he quietly knocked on the door to his girlfriend's bedroom, and Grandma appeared in the hall to scold him. "Get back to da couch, boy."

Laugh with the rest of the family when your cousin pouts, reliving this moment. When he says his grandmother lived her faith both inside and outside of the home, and she wanted the same of her family, understand that the small mercies your cousin has given in his life, he has given because of her.

18) Take a drink for each male cousin you see cry for the first time:

Kea, who once begged your mom to take him to California with her; who was for so many years your mom's favorite, even if she never admitted to it; of whom your grandmother made a hānai grandson because Kea's dad, her neighbor's son, was a mean alcoholic and Kea's body proved it. During the viewing, he whispers, "Tūtū, my Tūtū," as he gazes down at the body. He sobs when they close the casket. He is a pallbearer, one gloved hand lifting the casket, the other wiping his eyes, hidden behind dark glasses.

Your older cousin, Jason, who was the only person you trusted to teach you to ride a bike. You were seven. He was thirteen and beautiful. A ringer for King Kamehameha. He touches the casket gently, lets his fingers rest on its glossed wood. Like Kea, he is wearing sunglasses. His shoulders tremble with emotion. Later, in the evening, he teases you about buying your first surfboard at twenty-eight, and you tell him that you would have bought one sooner if he gave surf lessons. He laughs at that, and his laughter is a balm.

Finally, your baby cousin Ryan, who is no longer a baby, but a sophomore in high school. He is one of the great-grandchildren. He's lost weight since he was jumped at the end of his freshman year, got mean lickins, his arm broken. He is six foot one and, despite the weight loss, still muscled in a way that belies his teenage scrawniness. You forget how young he is sometimes. He says he doesn't remember how he got home last night. You want to tell him not to end up like some of his friends. You want to tell him he's smarter and better at baseball and masculine in a way no fifteen-year-old boy has any business being. He has that calm rage about him that scares you, that makes you want to hug him, that makes you respect him.

When Ryan helps carry the casket to the bed of the truck where the gravediggers are waiting, he, too, is crying. He, too, is using those clean white gloves to wipe his face. He comes to stand near you, and because you want to cry each time you see a man like that crying, you wrap your arms around his waist and lean into him. You let him be a man. You let yourself be a woman who needs his strength.

19) Take a drink for each cousin who brings his fighting cocks to the burial. Be thankful the birds remain in their cages, left in·the shade of so many tarp-covered F-150 truck beds.

20) Return to the mortuary for lunch and notice that the crowd of 200 has dwindled to a more manageable 125. Take a sip each time an auntie urges her homemade dessert on you: sweet potato manju, strawberry layer cake, chocolate mochi, guava Jell-O squares.

21) For the remainder of the day, take a drink every time a distant cousin asks how you're related to the deceased. Why didn't you remember to introduce yourself? Now three-quarters of the guests think you work for the mortuary and keep asking you where extra toilet paper is kept. (Point them to the hall cupboard.)

22) Take a drink when your uncles pull their trucks up to the side of the mortuary and haul out the big plastic coolers filled with beer.

23) Take a drink for each boy cousin who, upon finishing his lunch, drifts out to join the uncles. The men
are leaning against the side of a warehouse adjacent to the
mortuary, trying to squeeze into the sliver of shadow the
building provides. Their wives/girlfriends/baby-mamas
are still inside, talking story. Your aunties are cleaning,
placing fresh foil over the aluminum trays of kālua pig and
laulau, and carefully loading paper plates with food for
each neighbor or friend to take home.

Your uncles and aunties have so many friends—from
high school, work, the old neighborhood where they
grew up—who have come to support them. A few of the
friends didn't even know your grandmother, but they are
still here for your family. They are hugging your aunties,
pressing your uncles' hands, kissing your cousins on the
cheek. They are hānai.

Call them uncle, auntie. Kiss them. When they ask
whose girl you are, say, "Kanoa's. You know, Emma's eldest boy."

When they say, "Ho, I neva see 'im fo' long time,"
point your dad out to them. He's with the other men.
They leave you, as if in a trance, to go to him, hug him,
press his hand in theirs. "Look jus' like you, da daughta,"
they tell your dad, and he nods proudly.

24) Follow your cousins out to the mortuary parking lot. The sliver of shade from the neighboring warehouse has widened. The men are louder now, teasing each
other. Take a drink for every story that ends with your

dad's younger brother, Junior, getting lickins. And for the one that involved a homemade bomb and a telephone booth. "I like get all dat change," your uncle says, defending himself.

Another uncle, the one who will lose his job when the G&R Sugar Mill closes in six months, busts up. "Jus' like you. Find plenny ways fo' get paid." Laugh with all of them.

25) Take a drink for all the stories that compare Junior to his father, your grandfather. Take a drink for every car they restored, every beer they drank together, every football game where your grandpa cheered on Junior.

26) Take a drink when you realize your dad is not part of these stories.

27) Take a drink each time an auntie tells you your dad was not like your uncle. He was not like *any* of your uncles. He was the quiet one. The sweet one. The one who never made pilikia. He was the one who left.

28) Take a drink when they say you take after him.

29) Understand your dad was different from the outset. Hand him a beer. After all, to be a boy and to diverge; to watch football but not play it; to keep the books for your grandpa's market instead of unloading the trucks; to leave the island for boarding school; to want to go to college on the mainland; to want to stay there, on the mainland, with only one child to his name, and a girl at that, is to cease to want what men want. Your father is absent from your uncles' stories not because he left, but because

he was never of Kaua'i in the first place. Because he was in his own world. Because he is Hawaiian, but no local.

30) Take a drink because it's dark now and you didn't even notice. You have been awake since before dawn, at the mortuary by 7:30 a.m. You have been in mourning for two weeks, and now the funeral is over. The burial is done. Junior, the son whom everyone knows, has opened up his backyard to the family and extended families, and because it's Kaua'i, this could include more than a third of the island. Rachel, his wife, has put out the plastic card tables in one long row. The uncles sit beside the tables. A second row of chairs provides seating for the adult cousins. Junior's daughter and her husband sit in the outer circle. Auntie Miki, a real tita, like her mom—your grandmother's sister—is there, too. She sits with the men, in that inner circle.

Stay with the rest of the women, hovering around the exterior row of chairs, coming and going through the kitchen. Outside the house, the men have their food. Inside the house, your younger cousins are watching the Tupac biopic.

31) Drink a beer to wash down the raw crab in chili pepper sauce, the dried ahi, the tripe stew, the squid in coconut milk, the sashimi your uncle made from a filet of ono one of his friends gave him. Poi, chicken long rice, mochi, and lilikoi cake from the neighbors are placed in front of the men. One tray of Chinese noodles has spoiled.

It doesn't matter. Food covers three dining tables, and these are just the leftovers from lunch.

Junior is holding his Shih Tzu in his lap. Her leather collar has "Baby" printed on it in rhinestones. He is snagging a piece of pork katsu with his chopsticks and feeding bits of fried meat to the dog.

32) Take a shot of Crown Royal because someone found it in Junior's refrigerator and someone else has brought a second bottle and they're starting to run low on Bud Light, though there's still plenty of Heineken left. "Da Napilis, yoa grandma's side, neva drink, dem," your dad tells you. "But da Pakeles. Ho!"

"I know I one Pakele den," Junior says, laughing. He hands your dad a beer.

33) Drink, but do not call your mom. Do not call her even though you know she is missing everyone and wants to know what is happening. Do not call her, all the way in California, even though you said you would. When your auntie calls her, do not ask for the phone, but help pass it around so the other uncles and aunties can say something. Tomorrow you will talk to your mother. Tomorrow you will describe everything. But tonight this is yours. Do not share it. She should have come if she wanted to be a part of it so badly. She would have come if she had been thinking like a Hawaiian and not a haole.

34) Seek out your female cousins, the ones who used to pile onto that rattan chair with you. Squeeze next to

Johnell and her husband on the wooden bench, its blue paint peeling on the edges. Accept the beer Johnell hands you. Across from you sits Emmy, the one named for your grandmother, and her husband.

Your cousin Ryan hovers behind the bench. Scoot to make room for him to sit even though he refuses. He busies himself with his phone, but he remains behind you, waiting. Understand he has come to listen to you talk. After all, who knows what you might say? Who knows what someone like you thinks of all this?

Johnell and her husband start to poke fun at the pastor, but Emmy's husband stops them. He says the sermon was good. He liked it. "That sermon was serious," he says, and Ryan nods. His lean face is thoughtful.

But Johnell will have none of it. She's a teacher at Sacred Hearts Academy in Honolulu, so she knows something about sermons, and this one, she says, was crap. "I didn't need to think about hell. I was in it!"

Start to laugh—you couldn't agree more—but then notice Ryan watching you, like he expects an answer from you. Take a sip from your bottle to stall. Try to say something about the goodness of God, about forgiveness, about the pastors you've known who have given their own income to help support their parish. Instead, blurt out: "I don't trust men with manicures."

Everybody laughs, even Emmy and her husband, and Ryan most of all. He looks at you with a hint of admiration. Suspect that you, too, are leading him astray.

35) When your auntie calls you inside to see photos of your grandparents, take a long pull from the beer bottle. You did not know your grandfather. He died almost forty years ago, when your dad was twenty. Your dad kept no photographs of his father. In fact, you have never seen a picture of your grandfather. Now, the black-and-whites reveal a man with broad shoulders, a puffy face. He pulls more Chinese than you expected. In one picture he is laughing, and his eyes are tight and small. This is how your father laughs. This is how you laugh.

36) Take a shot when one of the women gets so drunk she announces her husband is screwing a Korean. Take another shot when the woman calls the mistress a yobo. Find out the drunk woman is a distant cousin. Her husband is a cousin, too, but from the other side of the family. No one claims the yobo.

37) Drink when the fighting cocks start crowing in their truck beds. Hear their cries echo throughout the neighborhood and a dozen dogs howl in sympathy. No one else seems to notice the commotion. The men still talk story, the women still pack plates of food. You are alone in your listening.

38) Take a drink when your cousin Mano, the one whose brother fights MMA, says he'll see you out at Bowls. When he smiles his teeth glint against his deep brown skin. He'll tell the other guys to let you catch some waves. He'll tell the other guys you're his cuz. He'll take care of you, and you know what this means: You are no

longer some Honolulu hapa. You are a Napili. You have one more name, another branch of family to whom you belong. One more from which you can't escape. Perhaps you are not your father after all. "Come see me now, yeah?" Mano says.

39) When you finally make up your mind to depart, do not take a drink. Do not let your dad take a drink. Hand him the keys to the car. He has had only three beers, maybe four, and is at least eight or nine behind the other men. Watch through the window as the resort condos of Poipu give way to Kaua'i's last remaining cane fields. Even in the dark, you can see the tendrils of smoke rising from where cane trash has been burning. The air smells acrid and sweet, like toasted orange rind. Flakes of ash fall and cling to your arms, sticky with a day's worth of sweat. You smell like you've been crying. You smell like beer.

Understand that your grandmother is in heaven now, and heaven has fighting cocks and Heineken, poi and dried ahi, your uncles' teasing and your aunties' cooking and your cousins laughing with you when you talk. Heaven is them acting like this is where you belong, and if that's what haole pastors call hell, then thank God you finally got here.

PORTRAIT OF A GOOD FATHER

The photograph hung for years in the screened-in porch beside their family kitchen. Even in Sarah's earliest recollections, the image is faded from sunlight: her father's deep brown skin has taken on a grayish hue, the white plumeria around his neck appears to have withered and yellowed, and his black, wavy hair is frosted with white. Humidity has caused the photograph to curl from its backing and bubble slightly in its gilded frame, lending the impression that Keaka is turning toward her.

In the photograph, Sarah's father is nineteen. He is a little thick in the middle, and his hair has already begun to withdraw from its original line like an army in retreat. But he is unmistakably handsome: his ali'i nose, flat and wide—the nose of King Kalākaua's line—flares slightly; his full lips are set in a mysterious smile; his chest is broad and hairless with dark, tight nipples. He is squinting slightly into the sun, and the photographer has caught him at a moment of introspection, at an angle, so Sarah can see his left earlobe.

Sarah will spend many hours staring at the photograph while she waits for her father: waits for him to cook her oatmeal before school, to figure out her math homework so he can explain it to her, to come home for dinner, or dessert, or afterward, when it's time to put her to bed. During these hours of waiting, she will memorize the lines of her father's neck, the way he tilts his head to the side as if falling into the sunlight, the smile that teases his lips. She will study the curve of his eyebrows, thick like hers, and the bulge of his biceps, similar to her older brother's. She will know the photograph as intimately as she knows her own self.

In later years, when she is in college on the mainland, and her roommates ask for a description of her parents—she has brought no pictures of them, only pictures of her high school friends—she will describe her father as he appeared in that photograph, at nineteen, before she was born.

Grace is five months pregnant with their first child when she photographs Keaka. They are at the beach and she is eating a peanut butter and jelly sandwich when she notices how the afternoon light catches in his black hair and makes his skin appear to glow from within. She has a camera with her and the lei Keaka bought her that morning when he stopped at the grocery store for more of the fruit preserves she likes.

She tosses him the lei. "Wear it," she commands as she turns on the camera. He sticks out his tongue, and she snaps a picture. He smiles, slightly embarrassed at the attention, and she takes another.

"Das enough now," he says. She lowers her right hand and rests it, still gripping the camera, on the beach blanket. She pretends to ignore him, picks up the sandwich with her left hand, and takes a bite. As Keaka turns to look at the ocean, Grace lifts the camera to her eye.

When at last Grace can slip into the white silk dress she has chosen as her wedding gown, she marries Keaka. John, their son, is already ten months old, and Grace's breasts are heavy with milk. But her waist is almost back to its original size, her stomach relatively flat, and the silk bodice clings kindly to her curves.

The wedding is held on Wilhelmina Rise, at Grace's parents' house, on their spacious balcony, which is built into the steep incline of the hillside. The couple say their vows with Diamond Head and the high-rise hotels of Waikīkī as a backdrop, and when the pastor proclaims them man and wife, an ambulance siren can be heard wailing in the distance as if in celebration. Keaka's aunties make all the food for the reception, even the three-layer mango wedding cake, and his uncles bring cases of beer and raw oysters from Costco. Grace's family brings wedding gifts: oversized boxes filled with silverware and porcelain plates.

In the living room, the Steelers' game is on television, and the groomsmen have loosened their ties, found a cooler filled with beer, and camped out on the couches. Keaka is in the center, his tie off, his black dress shoes lost in the jumble of slippers on the front porch. John-Boy sleeps in his father's arms while Grace greets her guests and thanks everyone for coming. She does not ask Keaka to join her in the tedium of hosting, but she resents his easy way of settling into her parents' home with his friends, with their son, while she, alone, is left to kiss all the aunties and hug all the uncles and say "we" thank you and "we" love you and "we," "we," "we."

For their wedding night, Grace and Keaka book a room at the Moana Surfrider Hotel in Waikīkī, where all the haole newlyweds vacation. They are alone for the first time in ten months: John-Boy is staying with Grace's parents. Keaka is still a little drunk from the reception, but Grace insists on having a mai tai beneath the huge banyan tree that spreads its limbs over the hotel's outdoor courtyard. They sit in silence while they wait for their drinks. They both watch the ocean, its white-tipped waves breaking loudly on the beach beside them, and then they drink the mai tais, also in silence. Grace can't understand why, but she feels sad, and she misses her baby. Her breasts are sore, even though she fed John-Boy before leaving her parents' house, and she worries her milk is staining the lining of the silk wedding dress.

They finish their mai tais and charge the drinks to the room, and just as they are standing to walk back to the covered porch, a rainstorm blows out from Mānoa Valley. The water comes in sheets and the air smells of tuberose. Grace begins to cry, but Keaka doesn't notice, for the rain is everywhere, and he's already brushing her hair from her eyes and pulling her sopping dress over her head. They make love on the bed, their wet clothes in a pile on the beige carpet.

They conceive Sarah, and for the rest of her life Grace will associate the scent of tuberose with profound sadness.

Sometimes, after hula on Saturday mornings, Sarah's dad picks her up from class and takes her to the beach. This has been their occasional tradition for three years now, since Sarah was seven. When she climbs into his truck, she slides across the bench seat and curls up next to him. She kisses his cheek and takes a deep breath. Her dad's hair is still damp from a shower, and he smells clean, like Ivory soap. But beneath this Sarah can smell other scents—beer, cologne, pikake flower—she isn't supposed to know.

Often when she emerges from the dim lights of her hula hālau, Sarah can see two figures outlined in the tinted windows of the truck: Keaka and John-Boy. If this is the case, then when Sarah heaves herself into the truck she smells mildew and dirty feet, she smells boy.

These Saturday excursions are bittersweet. Keaka only takes them to the beach when he doesn't make it for dinner the night before and is in deep trouble with their mom. He only takes them to the beach when he doesn't want to be at home.

On the way to the ocean, they pick up Spam musubi from 7-Eleven or, if Sarah and John-Boy are really hungry, loco moco from Rainbow Drive-In. They sit in the truck, doors open to catch the breeze, and pop the egg yolks in their loco moco to watch the yellow bleed into the gravy and rice. Sarah doesn't like the hamburger meat, so she divvies up the patties: one for her brother, one for her dad.

Keaka asks Sarah how hula class was and she describes the difficulty of making her knees lift when she tries to 'uwehe or how, when she raises her arms to show the pali, she always forgets to tuck in her elbows. Her kumu says she makes a mountain with wings.

Her dad laughs, but not unkindly. "No worries, you remember next time," he tells her cheerfully. "Why lif' da knees so high? No need. Stay low to da ground." His hints feel like guesses, and part of her questions how he knows to guide her like this, he who has never danced, but somehow his advice always turns out to be right.

At the beach, she changes into her swimsuit and lies

in the sand until she is so hot she wonders if the sand has come alive and crawled on top of her. Rivulets of sweat run down her arms and chest. When she can bear the heat no longer, she springs up, sand raining down on John-Boy, and races toward the water. She can hear John-Boy behind her and then their dad huffing a little with the sudden exertion. John-Boy is yelling at her that he's going to win, and she yells back, "I'm almost there."

But, as always, she hesitates at the water's edge. John-Boy bolts past her, jumps into the water, and swims without fear toward the breaking waves. She feels her shoulders slump with disappointment. Behind her, Keaka sighs and says, "You beat me again." She knows he's only saying this to make her feel better, but she likes to hear it all the same. Good fathers know when to lie to their children.

While John-Boy can jump into the water without fear, Sarah will enter the ocean only if she is clinging to her dad's back, arms wrapped tightly around his neck, and legs tucked beneath his arms. He lets the waves lash at him, splashing to either side of his body as the spray tickles her feet. She turned ten two months ago and knows she is getting too old for this sort of special treatment, but she feels safe clinging to her father's back, hidden behind him. Once they are outside of the crash zone, he paddles, and she lets her legs float behind her. He tells her when to hold her breath because they are going to dive underwater, and he reminds her to start breathing again when they come up, as if she might forget. Underwater, the sun feels cool and blue. Her father's skin is warm as the sand. She can hear his heart beating, slow and steady.

One quiet Saturday afternoon in February, when the sun hangs lazily near the horizon, and the earth smells damp and green after a night of rain, Keaka pulls his truck in front of the hula studio, and he is not alone. At first, when Sarah comes running out the door and sees the shadowed outline of two people sitting behind the tinted glass, she assumes her brother's baseball game has ended early. But then the passenger door swings open and a small Korean woman descends. She is wearing black sandals with heels and a flower-print dress belted fashionably around her waist. She is completely out of place at the hula school, where all the other women are wearing jeans or cotton shorts and T-shirts. Keaka steps out of the truck and motions toward the woman. "Sarah, this is my friend Joon."

"I have heard so much about you." Joon bends down to kiss Sarah on the cheek.

Sarah smiles shyly. Joon is beautiful, with a face shaped like a diamond: wide at the high cheekbones and angled at the chin. Her skin is the white of coconut milk and her lips are painted a brilliant, daring red. In Joon's beauty and careful dress, her fashion and precise English, she is completely foreign. Sarah has never met a woman like this, and she wonders how Keaka might have come across her.

In the truck, seated between her father and Joon, Sarah asks, "You come with us to the beach, Auntie?"

Joon laughs, and her laughing is like a gasp. "No, not me. I burn too easily."

"You like come Rainbow Drive-In then?"

Joon shakes her head. "Your dad is just dropping me off at home. I needed a ride."

Sarah stops asking questions and, leaning slightly against Joon, stares out the window. Joon giggles and rests her hand on Sarah's head. Keaka drives them to the back of Mānoa Valley, where a wet mist still sits on the finger-shaped leaves of mango and plumeria trees. When Joon exits the car, she leaves behind the scent of jasmine. She ascends a steep driveway and turns to wave. Sarah waves back eagerly.

Keaka drives next to Mānoa Park, where John-Boy's Little League game is in its last inning. John-Boy has just come up to bat. He swings and misses on the first pitch, but on the second, he hits a line drive up left field that bounces off the tip of the third baseman's glove. John-Boy stops at second base. "How you know Auntie Joon?" Sarah curls up beside her dad, and he drapes his arm around her shoulders.

"Work."

"She looks like one fashion model. I like her belt."

"Like one model," Keaka repeats. Sarah feels her head bounce softly against her father's chest as he chuckles. "But say, no tell yoa mom 'bout Auntie Joon. Dey no get along."

Sarah is about to ask why they don't get along when Robert Kenui, John-Boy's best friend, hits a ball far into right field. John-Boy starts running, and he is like a mongoose, speeding around the diamond. He rounds third, then heads for home. Keaka is yelling at him through the truck's windshield. "Go, son. Go for it!"

Sarah is up in her seat, screaming, "Run, John."

The right fielder throws the ball to first to get Robert out. The first baseman throws home. But John-Boy slides across home base just as the ball hits the catcher's mitt. "Safe!" yells Keaka. "The boy is safe!" John-Boy's team wins the game.

In the truck after the game John-Boy retells the story of sliding into home. "Because I made the sacrifice," Robert interrupts. "Because of me." Sarah and her brother are sharing a seat belt in the center of the bench while Robert has the passenger side. Keaka keeps asking the boys if they thought they were going to make it or not, and they keep changing their answer. "I thought I was," says Robert, and then, later, "No, I knew I had to sacrifice for John-Boy to get home."

They drive all the way to Sandy's on the east side of the island because the boys want to bodysurf and Keaka is feeling generous. At the beach, Sarah and the boys change into their swimsuits in the bathroom. Sarah hates the beach bathrooms, with their cement flooring where the water pools and their unflushed toilets. In one toilet, the water is dark red with blood, and Sarah wonders how someone can bleed that much and not die.

Outside of the restrooms, she and her brother wait

for Robert. He is carefully applying sunscreen, using the metal tablets that serve as mirrors to see if he's missed any spots on his face. Sarah thinks of Joon, the shininess of her black belt, and the way her dress moved like water across her skin. "I met one friend of Dad's today," Sarah says. John-Boy looks up from the scab on his knee he's been picking but doesn't answer her.

"She was so pretty," she adds. John-Boy frowns and Sarah senses she has said something wrong. "Joon is a friend of Dad's from work," she tries to explain. "She needed a ride home."

John-Boy glares at Sarah and opens his mouth to speak, but at that moment Robert emerges from the bathroom, his pale skin now white with sunscreen, and his belly waggling slightly as he jogs to them. "You better not say nothing to Mom," John-Boy whispers angrily before he and Robert run to the water.

Sarah wants to ask her dad why John-Boy is mad at her, and why her mom shouldn't hear about Joon. Sarah remembers wanting a purple satin nightgown from Sears and her mother flatly refusing to buy it for her. Sarah suspects that women like Joon sleep in nothing but purple satin.

Sarah knows she is getting too big to ride on her father's back, but she insists he take her beyond the break all the same. She gets him to agree by promising to ride in a wave on her own, without holding on. He has tried to teach her to let the whitewash buoy and carry her, like a thousand hands, toward the shore, and how and when to dive under a wave, her head and body deep enough to slip unharmed beneath the break even as her feet remain near the surface, tickled by the swirling wash.

In the water, she climbs on his back, and he paddles out with her. At first she wraps her arms around his neck, but he says she's choking him, so she moves her hands to his shoulders and digs her fingers into the soft indentations above his collarbones. They dive together beneath the first wave, Keaka telling her to hold her breath and then saying when it's safe to breathe again. A second wave breaks close behind the first, and Sarah takes a deep breath. When they dive beneath the lip of the wave, she sticks her head up, like a turtle, to feel the water lift and twirl her hair.

But she miscalculates the water's strength. The wave lifts her off her father's back and pushes her down, breaking on top of her. Without knowing which way is up or down, she flails. She opens her eyes, but the water is cloudy with churned sand. She swims for a murky patch of light and breaks the surface of the water as yet another wave crashes down. This time she doesn't have a chance to catch her breath, and the wave rolls her over and over like a tumbleweed in a Wile E. Coyote cartoon. She has been told once, while hiking, that if she loses her way, she should stay in one place and wait to be found. She wishes to apply that logic now. Her father will be looking for her. Can't she just wait for him?

Her lungs burn and she can feel the ocean sucking back

the water and building into another wave. She knows she will drown if she waits for help. She swims toward the light again, and when she breaks the surface, she is facing a steep wall of water. She takes a deep breath and dives beneath it.

She struggles through the waves until, finally, she is outside of the break zone. When she spots her dad, he is frantically looking for her, calling her name, diving under water, as if she could be seen in the haze. He is outside of the waves, though, and Sarah feels betrayed, as if he hasn't tried hard enough to find her. Shouldn't he know she'd be caught on the inside in the mess of the break zone?

Back on shore, as he wraps her in a towel and hugs her, she studies him. His brow is creased with concern, his eyes watery from the salt. She wants him to tell her the things she doesn't yet know. "Joon doesn't have kids, yeah," she says.

Keaka leans back from her, his hands still gripping her upper arms, and stares at her, a little surprised. "No. No keiki."

"She doesn't work construction. Cannot if she like dress how she like dress."

"She no work construction," Keaka confirms. Sarah feels like a hypnotist: the way Keaka watches her is how she's seen people on television watch a pocket watch on a chain. "She's a good friend, yeah."

Sarah wants to push him further, wants him to tell her that Joon is the reason Keaka does not come home on Friday nights, that she makes him forget dinner or his promise to watch a movie with Sarah and John-Boy or tell her a story before bed. Sarah does not know what Joon has that she, Keaka's daughter, does not, but Sarah does understand jealousy, and some part of her understands how to make her father feel bad for making her feel bad. She sits quietly on the warm sand. "I just wish you'd come home when you say you will."

Keaka recoils, his hands dropping from her shoulders as if her skin has burned them. Sarah is instantly sorry for what she has said. She has damaged something between them, hurt her father in a way she didn't mean to. Instead of earning his trust, she has loosened the small, tightly woven cord that holds them together against the world of whitewash and rogue waves and brothers who always beat her into the ocean. Suddenly, Sarah understands she will no longer be invited to ride on her father's back, and that their Saturday afternoons at the beach are numbered.

When John-Boy and Robert return from the water, Keaka tells the kids to pack up. They are going home. "So early?" John-Boy whines. Keaka shoots him a cold look, and John-Boy knows enough to turn accusingly to Sarah and whisper, "What'd you do?" Sarah does not answer. She's not sure what she did, but she knows what she wanted: for her dad to belong wholly and completely to her family.

⌒

Her entire life Grace has suspected men know things because they think them, and women know things because they feel them. She cannot describe her philosophy any better than that. She just knows that men and women are different in how they come upon knowledge, and women do not need to witness something to know it has happened.

This is why, on December 15 at 3:42 p.m., when her cell phone vibrates in her blazer pocket, Grace senses the world is not right. She has been counting twenties for Mr. Osaka, an elderly Japanese gentleman who has banked with Central Pacific for more than fifteen years, and who always remembers to ask Grace about her children. Grace stops between two hundred and two hundred and twenty, sets the bills down, and answers her phone. Mr. Osaka watches her, confused, concerned.

Mary, another teller, stops what she is doing the moment she hears the high note of alarm in Grace's voice. "Why aren't the kids at your house, Momma?" Mr. Osaka's unfinished transaction blinks on Grace's computer screen. He bows his head and stares, without seeing, at the pile of bills on the counter in front of him. He moves his hand forward, as if to hold Grace's, and then stops himself. Mary waves him on to the next available window and turns her back to the growing line of people waiting to cash their mid-month paychecks.

Grace is aware that while Mr. Osaka and Mary cannot hear what's being said on the other end of the line, they can hear her responses, and she offers them a tight smile. "I'm at work, Momma. The kids were supposed to be at your house this afternoon. I'll call John-Boy's cell." Grace hangs up the phone.

Grace steps into the glass meeting room behind the teller windows. As her son's phone rings, she watches Mary finish counting Mr. Osaka's bills. Mary apologizes to him for the interruption. Mr. Osaka bows toward Mary, and then he looks at Grace, gazing at her through the soundproof glass of the office, and bows again. His expression is one of deep pity, and panic rises in Grace's chest. She feels as if Mr. Osaka can see something she cannot.

When John-Boy doesn't answer his cell, Grace tries her husband. "No, I at work," Keaka shouts. "Why I go pick 'em up?"

"Don't yell at me. I merely want to know where the kids are."

"Maybe dey wen go fo' shave ice on da way. No can reach 'em on John-Boy's cell?" Keaka shuffles something on the other end of the line, and Grace pictures him at his desk with a stack of invoices. He's always grumpy when he's paying bills.

"I tried already. No answer."

"You wen tell 'em go Tūtū's house, yeah?" Despite his calm voice, she can't help but feel he's blaming her for this.

"They know the routine." She tries to remember if,

that morning, she told them to wait for her at school. With Christmas coming, she's been picking them up more often than usual so they can run errands with her, buy gifts for the grandparents, bake cookies for a classroom party, stop by the Ben Franklin craft store for an end-of-term science project. She wants to believe she misspoke this morning and told them not to walk to their grandmother's house. She wants to believe that whatever mistakes she's made, they'll be the kind she can easily fix. "Maybe they're waiting for me at school. Or maybe John-Boy went to a friend's house and Sarah is watching the boys play video games or maybe . . ." Grace shakes her head, frustrated with herself. "But if they were waiting at school for me, John-Boy would have called. And if John-Boy went off with his friends, he'd make sure Sarah was with one of us."

"Sarah? Da girl missing?"

"I don't know where either of them are. I just told you that!" She shouts. Keaka only hears pieces of what she says, never all of it.

Grace hears more shuffling on the other end of the line, and then a small cough. "I gon drive to da school fo' try see 'em walking home." The phone taps against Keaka's cheek as if it's bouncing as he jogs to his truck. "I gon call you soon." His voice is gentle, whispered, like he's telling her a secret. His voice is so unexpectedly tender that she will remember it long after the rest of the day has sunken into a dark blur.

In the back of Mānoa Valley, the rain is falling heavily, and Joon listens to it drum against the roof of her 'ohana. She has nestled herself beside Keaka's chest, her nose an arrow to his nipple, her mouth against his rib. Her breath gathers damply against his skin, and she can feel the moisture echoed back on her upper lip.

Her studio has no curtains or shades, but the little building is set on the back of her parents' property and surrounded by avocado trees, so it stays cool and dark and private. She likes her space, the rattan floor mats, the sliding screen that separates the bed from the living room, the kitchenette off to the side of the entrance. She likes that this belongs to her, that she can share it at her will. Keaka has his house, his wife, his family. And she has her 'ohana, which belongs to her alone. Sometimes she refuses to let him inside, declines to see him, a reminder of the power she can wield. Other days she is grateful to see the outline of his body beneath her sheets, to hear him humming in her shower, to see him cooking on her little hot plate.

At thirty-two, Joon is a secretary in a law office downtown, and she prides herself on her good sense. She understands Keaka will not leave Grace as long as the children are still living at home, and she has had her own dalliances in the years she and Keaka have been together. She once went an entire year without him, before running into him again by chance—he was at her favorite club, waiting for her it seemed—and falling back into old habits.

She has, at times, wondered how long their affair can last, the roller coaster of on and off and on again, but by now they've spent more than thirteen years together, and at times she wonders if they will continue like this for the rest of their lives. In more sober moments, she hopes to find a man who wants to marry her, or whom she wants to marry, and then she will drop Keaka forever, and he will understand what it feels like to need, not just desire.

If pressed, she would admit she cannot picture this future husband of hers. She cannot even create the smallest details of his face because, for her to love him, he would have to have Keaka's mouth, and if his mouth, then why not his eyes and nose and the curve of his brow line? And this man—this future husband—would need to dance with her as Keaka does, holding her so tightly that each breath is pained. He must make her breakfast like Keaka does, remembering she likes her eggs over easy with fried onions and cold rice. And he would have to make love to her as Keaka does, sometimes roughly, with the old excitement of their youth, and sometimes with such gentleness she yearns to cry. Sometimes she feels sorry for this future husband of hers, who will always be compared to Keaka and found lacking, and having felt pity, she then is content again to be with Keaka.

She is lightly running her fingers along his bare arm

when his cell phone rings. She sees the caller ID: Grace. He moves to turn the phone off, but Joon rolls away from him. "Just answer her," she says. Her daydreams have been interrupted, and now she wants to get on with the realities of the day.

Joon can hear Grace's voice blasting through the phone: "Do you have the kids?"

Keaka turns down the volume. "No, I at work. Why I go pick 'em up?" He digs his free hand under the covers and rests it on Joon's naked hip. She doesn't brush him away. As he tells Grace to check with her mom, his hand crawls along the curve of Joon's hipbone, toward her pubic area, to the edge of her hair. She pushes the blankets off her naked body, shuffling the crisp sheets.

"You wen tell 'em go Tūtū's house, yeah?" Keaka asks. He nestles his fingers in the folds of Joon's labia. She is already wet. He strokes her softly. Keaka's probing fingers, the daring of their affair, even Grace's muffled voice on the phone have conspired to turn her on. Joon arches her back.

Suddenly, Keaka stops. He pulls his hand away and wipes his fingers, unthinking, on the pillowcase. Joon slaps his stomach, annoyed.

"Sarah?" he says. "Da girl missing?"

Joon pauses, sorry for slapping him. She knows how devoted Keaka is to his children, the kind of father he is. She can hear the worry in his voice.

The children are the one area of their affair that does not please Joon. Even when she dismisses Grace in her mind, Joon cannot remove the children. She feels, from a distance, an affection for those children, Keaka's children. Sarah's big and wondering eyes; John-Boy's aloofness, like his father, that one. If she were allowed, Joon would love them as she loves Keaka. She would claim them as her own. They are that beautiful.

Now they are missing, or Sarah is missing, and Joon can do nothing because, in the end, she is just the woman with whom Keaka is having an affair. She is neither friend nor aunt. She is no mother figure. She is nothing.

Keaka springs from Joon's bed. He tries to dress quickly, hopping to pull his jeans over his hips, and the phone jiggles between his shoulder and ear.

Joon is watching him, questioning with her furrowed eyebrows. He looks at her apologetically. He shakes his head, refusing to answer her implied questions. "I gon call you soon," he promises.

Sarah and John-Boy always walk the long way to their grandmother's house because going that way with Robert is better than taking the shortcut by themselves. Robert's house is on the same side of Wai'alae Avenue as their middle school, so they skip the guarded crosswalk and wait to dart across Wai'alae when they reach Robert's. From there, they cut over to Wilhelmina Rise.

The added benefit of walking Robert home is that Gordon Yu, a boy in Sarah's grade, lives across the street.

Gordon's mom picks him up from school, but she always runs late, so usually she is parking her minivan, Gordon safely ensconced inside, just as Sarah and John-Boy reach Robert's house. If Sarah hurries the boys slightly in their walk home, she can be passing Gordon's house just as he climbs from his mother's car. And Sarah can wave at him, perhaps pause for a brief chat about homework or P.E., before her brother pulls her away.

Gordon's house is painted a delicate yellow, the color of the wine Sarah's mother sometimes drinks with dinner. Sarah imagines that such a yellow would taste sweet and lemony all at once. She wonders if Gordon, too, might taste this way. Robert pulls on Sarah's ponytail. "I asked you what you're thinking," he says. She looks at him blankly. Have he and John-Boy been talking to her all this time?

"Leave her alone. She's tired." John-Boy smiles at her, that small, secret smile, the one that says he knows what she's thinking and won't tell, and Sarah smiles back.

Robert shrugs. "Beach tomorrow?"

"Yeah, if I no need go Christmas shopping with my mom." John-Boy makes a face, and Robert chuckles.

"You should see her." Sarah pretends to carry a stack of boxes in her arms. "I think they're for her, not us, but." The boys laugh.

John-Boy steps toward the curb, and Sarah stands beside him. Robert waits to watch them cross, which is part of the routine. Sarah looks down the street, toward Gordon's house. Mrs. Yu is climbing into the car, turning on the engine, preparing to back out of the driveway. Sarah feels her stomach sink. Mrs. Yu is later than usual, so no sightings today. She inches the car backward until her bumper is in the street, and then she pauses to see if any traffic is coming. Sarah spots a low-riding silver Honda come speeding off the highway and onto Wai'alae. She wonders if she can stall the boys until Mrs. Yu returns from picking up Gordon. Sarah turns to look at Robert, to ask him about the beach or eighth grade or anything, only to stay rooted there for a few more minutes until Gordon appears.

"My side is good. Let's go!" Sarah hears John-Boy call. He tugs her hand. She means to tug back, to hold him, but her fingers slip through his. The brake lights on Mrs. Yu's minivan light up red, and the vehicle bounces with the suddenness of its stop. The speeding Honda careens around the minivan's bumper. It doesn't slow. John-Boy's hand is no longer in Sarah's.

She should yell at her brother or grab his cotton shirt or throw herself in the way of the car, but all she can do is watch it curve around Mrs. Yu's minivan. Then, before she can finish turning her head toward the street, she hears a soft thump and knows, without looking, that this is the sound of her brother's body bouncing against the Honda.

The problem, Grace realizes, is that she remembers everything and Keaka nothing. When they lie in bed at night, without touching, neither reaching to hold nor speaking to the other, Grace lists the things Keaka has forgotten, as if in tallying her husband's erasures she might better rebuild the memory of their son. Grace knows that Keaka no longer recalls his drive to the children's school, nor her phone call to him as he arrived in the parking lot. He has no memory of the hospital, no vision of the tubes that wound like complicated piping around the still body of John-Boy. Keaka does not remember the next morning when John-Boy died, nor the funeral the following week when Grace watched Keaka absently greet his coworkers and friends at the service, as he shook hands and allowed his cheek to be kissed. All the time he looked at their friends and family members—the people who had populated their lives for years—as if they were strangers and his own actions were unrecognizable to him. He seemed to float blankly, while she was overwhelmed by everything, the sight of tuberose lei draped over the casket, and the apple scent of styling oil in John-Boy's molded hair, and the stiff feel of her son's earlobes, carefully reconstructed and slick as plastic.

Grace thinks Keaka has forgotten her, too. She wants him to look at her, to recognize her body, even as it becomes lighter, dropping off her like layers of fabric. And her skin, always pale, takes on a bluish transparency that frightens her. Keaka says nothing. He remains silent when the food on her plate goes uneaten, and when she shakes at night—not from cold or crying, but because her body has taken to shaking and she no longer controls it. Keaka refuses to see her, refuses to touch her. She no longer exists for him.

When the evening news describes the silver Honda, offers sketches of the two teenagers behind the wheel, Keaka stares blankly at the television screen. He seems incapable of connecting those men, that car, with the tragedy in his life—*their* life. Their son.

One day Grace overhears Keaka at the front door. He is speaking to another man, both their voices hushed, though the other voice—the unfamiliar one—is laden with grief and Keaka's is blank. Grace steps into the hallway. From here she can see the front door, and she recognizes the black dress shoes, the blue uniform. A policeman. She waits, leaning against the hallway wall, pressing her cheek against one of the children's drawings, which was taped to the wall years ago and then left there.

The policeman is saying the young men have been captured. Plenty of witnesses will help put them behind bars. Grace feels a sudden surge of rage. She wants to scream at the officer, at the boys, at the unfairness of the world. She steps toward the door, but then she hears Keaka: "Too bad, yeah," he's saying to the officer. "Kids nomo drive careful." He sounds lost, as if speaking out of a fog. Grace steps back into the hall's shadows again, her anger drained. Her husband is the voice of fog, she realizes, and as if in echo, the trade winds shift and volcanic ash blows from Big Island to O'ahu and the vog hangs in the air.

At night, when Grace and Keaka lie together without

touching or sleeping, they listen to Sarah cry. Sarah shows no emotion during the day—she is her father's daughter in that way—but at night, when she thinks she is alone, her desolation is tangible. Grace can bear it—can bear to share Sarah's grief in silence—but Keaka seems tortured by their daughter's sadness. He tosses and turns. He grips his pillow tightly to his ears, and still the crying continues. At dinner, two weeks after the funeral, he announces, "Nomo crying in dis house." He says this firmly, setting his fork down noisily on his plate. He doesn't look at Sarah, but at Grace, and Grace stares back at him.

At first she thinks to argue: Who is he to make an announcement such as this? Who is he to direct the progress of their mourning? But then Grace looks at their daughter. Sarah is pushing a piece of chicken from one end of her plate to the other. Her silence is dense, her body taking on the same slightness as her mother's. Perhaps Keaka is right. Perhaps a moratorium on crying is what Sarah needs.

"Nomo crying," Keaka says again.

Grace holds his gaze. She nods. "No more crying," she repeats.

Sarah says nothing.

Later that night, lying in bed, Grace is unnerved by the silence. The trade winds refuse to stir, leaves are moored to their trees, the neighborhood dogs have all crawled under porches and fallen asleep, and the cats have stalked off to find a different mate worth howling over. In the far distance, if she listens closely, Grace can hear the monotone buzz of traffic on the freeway. The night is heavy, suffocating. The vog sits immovable. In the silence, she wonders if Keaka misses their daughter's grief, if the sound of her crying was a reminder to him that he was still alive.

Sarah learns to tell the story the same way every time. The same pauses, the same lift of her voice at the part where her parents show up at the hospital, the same embarrassed glance downward when she describes telling Robert to call 911. She can recite the facts with minimal emotion, slowly, looking her listener in the eye: a cousin, a friend, and later, college roommates, new boyfriends. Over and over, the same small hitch in her voice when she says, "The car came out of nowhere." The same little tug on her right earlobe when she recounts riding in the ambulance.

"The story can be summed up in three words: hit and run." This is how she always opens. She hopes the lead-in conveys how John-Boy's death was completely unromantic, anticlimactic, dull. By retelling her story, she emphasizes the quotidian attributes of her loss. Who hasn't witnessed a fender-bender? Or felt sadness? Or despised the antiseptic smell of a hospital waiting room? She wants her listener to nod in recognition while she speaks. But she also hopes her audience finds her story completely incomprehensible.

She hates that John-Boy died in a hit-and-run. He was worthy of something grander, more impossible, more beautiful. The fact of his death is plain, and in its plainness, his death becomes real. At night, when Sarah cannot fall asleep, she dreams up better and more flamboyant fatalities for her brother: shark attack, helicopter crash in Mākaha Valley, kidnapping, being run over by an airplane taking off from Hickam Air Force Base (she finds the military adds a certain level of national intrigue), fatal head injury while surfing, skydiving (this one she has returned to often; she is fascinated by the idea of her brother shooting through space like a star), submarine failure, mine collapse, and a house fire into which he runs to save a young girl. Most other modes of death strike her as comparatively hopeful and lovely. She wishes he had died differently. She wishes anything except "the car came out of nowhere." But mostly she wishes John-Boy wasn't dead.

While Sarah completes her homework, Grace hovers nearby. In the year since John-Boy's death, Grace has become a moth, forever fluttering through the house, attracted to the light of John-Boy's memory. "Remember when he won this essay contest?" she says aloud as she dusts a small trophy that remains on a shelf in the family room. Sarah looks up from her homework and nods even though her mother doesn't turn to look at her. Sarah does remember when John-Boy won that contest. He wrote about the historical significance of Waikīkī to the ancient ali'i. He was only in seventh grade.

Grace has given away much of his clothing to the Goodwill, and his baseball equipment was gifted to the school, but the trophies, the unfinished homework, worksheets with gold star stickers circling his name, his pillowcases: these items are treasured, dusted, wiped down with care, and neatly laid to rest on shelves throughout the house. "He was such a good student," Grace sighs as she sits down on the couch to fold laundry, always in mid-conversation with an invisible companion.

Sarah's schoolwork also draws comments about John-Boy: "John-Boy never had to learn about relative pronouns." "John-Boy excelled at math." "John-Boy loved American history." Sarah understands that she, in life, will never measure up to her brother in death, and this seems right and good. Sarah comes to think of her brother as a sun. Everything he did shone with excellence.

After dinner, Keaka sits down next to Sarah at the kitchen table for their evening ritual: pre-algebra homework. This past week, though he has not slept at home, and he and Grace are barely speaking, he has remained late each evening to be with Sarah. She recognizes the devotion on her father's part, even if she doesn't understand why he cannot show this same tenderness toward her mother.

As usual, Sarah works through as many of the math problems as she can and then shows the rest to her father. Patiently, he explains how to solve the first of the unfinished equations. "You need divide on bot' sides da equals sign," he says. "What kine number you need?" Sarah smiles down at her homework. She loves the way her father's pidgin contrasts with his acute understanding of mathematics. For years, this duality reminded Sarah of a caterpillar: seemingly simple, but within itself something beautiful and grand.

"Three," she says, taking the pencil from him. She can feel him watching her intently. She can't remember John-Boy ever receiving this kind of attention from their dad. Keaka went to John-Boy's baseball games, school events, even teacher's meetings, but he never had the same patience with his son as he does with his daughter. Sarah almost feels undeserving of his interest, and she wishes he spoke of John-Boy more.

"Good. Now what you get?"

"Four. So x equals four?"

"Yes! Das it!" Her dad's excitement is expansive. Its energy swallows her whole.

"I get it now." She reaches her arms around his waist and squeezes, and her dad kisses the crown of her head.

"You like I stay watch you?"

"No need, Dad," she says, though she knows he likes to sit with her.

"You sure?" He makes no move to leave the table. She wants to forgive him for his attention. Like her mother, he tends to stay close these days. But Sarah feels frustrated with him. Her old excitement in him is diminished. The promise she once felt he possessed is gone. He has put on weight, become roly-poly in the middle, lost much of his hair. His eyes are lined with tiny creases, his once-illuminating grin has been condensed into a tight smile. He seems to crawl through life. She doesn't need him now as she once did.

"I'm fine," she says, bowing her head over her homework. Eventually he rises and leaves her in silence, and then she is sorry for dismissing him as she has.

An hour later, as Sarah brushes her teeth before bed, she hears her parents talking in their bedroom. Grace is putting away the folded laundry. Keaka is watching. "John-Boy used to finish his homework before ten p.m.," Sarah hears her mother say.

"But he neva work as hard as Sarah does. When he no get someting, he no do it. Sarah work t'rough da problems until she get evryting." Sarah can hear her father's pride.

"I wish you wouldn't compare them like that." Grace's voice is high-pitched and quavering. She is about to cry. "John-Boy was very good at school."

"He was. I know," Keaka says soothingly. The bed springs creak under his weight. "I jus' mean Sarah stay a hard worker. She really like try, her."

"Don't talk about my son like that. He was a hard worker too."

"I neva say John-Boy not a hard worker. I just wen say dat Sarah . . ." Keaka trails off. "Stop crying," he pleads. But Grace can never stop once she's started.

Sarah closes the bathroom door and stands behind it, listening. "You don't miss him," Grace sobs at Keaka. "You didn't love him like I did. He was the reason you had to stay with me."

"He neva was no reason fo' nutting. He was my son. I loved him." Sarah can picture her dad, his hands upturned in helplessness, his caterpillar face scrunched up in frustration.

"It doesn't matter. You would have treated her better than me no matter." Her hand slaps the wall and the flat sound echoes in the hallway.

"I tol' you neva bring her into dis." Someone closes the bedroom door so Sarah can't discern what else is being said, but she can still hear her parents' muffled voices rising and falling. In the mirror above the sink, Sarah studies her reflection. She is growing out of her childish looks. Her face is narrowing, her cheeks are less full, her chin slightly more pointed. She has the first hint of breasts poking from beneath the thin cotton of her nightshirt, and she can see, on her bare legs, the dark hair that has become embarrassing to her in the past two months.

"Stop!" Keaka yells suddenly. "Stop crying!"

"It would have been different if it was hers." Grace is screaming hysterically. Someone punches the wall, and the mirror in the bathroom shivers with the vibrations.

The bedroom door slams. Then the front door. Then her father's truck door. Sarah hears the engine growl awake. She sits on the closed toilet lid and leans her head against the wall. She focuses on the word "hers."

It would have been different if it was mine, Sarah says to herself, *my life that ended.* If John-Boy had lived instead, then perhaps her parents wouldn't fight as they do now. Perhaps her father would have grieved for Sarah more openly, and Grace would have forgiven him his faults, and John-Boy, who understood their parents in a way Sarah never has, would have comforted them as Sarah never could.

She hears a light tap on the bathroom door. She opens it hesitantly. Her mother is standing outside, eyes red-rimmed but dry. *If only I had been the one hit by the car and not John-Boy,* Sarah thinks. Grace takes Sarah into her arms and holds her. *If only it had been my life and not his.*

When he finally comes to Joon, Keaka has been driving in circles for hours, up the spiraling side streets of St. Louis Heights, and back down to the beach community of Kāhala. He has left Grace at last. Joon knows without him having to tell her. In truth, he has been in the process of leaving Grace for two weeks, since Joon told him she was pregnant. Sometimes Joon wonders if Keaka has actually been leaving Grace for years, since before Joon was pregnant, before John-Boy's funeral, even before Keaka's wedding, all those years ago, when he loved Grace enough to marry but not enough to remain faithful to her.

Even after Joon opens the front door, Keaka remains standing on her porch, without moving to come in, as if he is just dropping off a note or a piece of mail, and she has to take his arm and lead him into her 'ohana. He sits down on the edge of the bed, and she sits down beside him. He is shaken, but she can't understand by what or why. His leaving is not a surprise—not to her, not to him, not even to Grace, who has known about Joon and her baby for a week now.

Keaka doesn't speak. Joon asks, "So are you done talking things out with Grace?"

He nods. "She get plenny mad tonight. I tink, maybe I leave and we still be friends. Now I know I crazy fo' tink dat." He laughs without smiling. "You know, she said someting and I no stop tinking 'bout it."

Joon reaches out and folds her hand around his. She waits for him. With Keaka, silence is a form of dialogue.

"She wen said, 'It would have been different if it was hers.'" His choice of words is precise, his speech taking on Grace's cadence.

"I don't understand," Joon says. "If what was whose?"

"If it was yoa baby gone died. Our baby. If someting wen happen to ours, like happen to John-Boy. She tink I go treat you bettah. I stay wit' you. She tink, if da wors' happen fo' you and me, I gon care more."

"She said all that?" Joon crosses her arms, rigid with indignation.

"She said dat, and I tink, maybe she right. I neva gon

leave you, no matta what. But I tink, she not right when she say dese tings 'bout da kids. I love 'em, you know. Our baby I will love, but my Sarah." Keaka's voice quivers. "And John-Boy . . ." He does not continue, but Joon can finish the sentence for him.

"He was your son."

Keaka nods. "Nutting can replace dat."

"Not even our baby," Joon says, and her voice betrays more regret than she wishes. Keaka does not reply.

Joon knows Keaka wants her child. He has told her that he is excited to be a father again, and this time without the weight that Grace's pregnancies carried so many years ago, when he was tied to her and unable to escape his future. Keaka has said that this time around, with Joon, he feels light, eager, free.

When she first realized she was pregnant, Joon told Keaka he could stay or go. She would make it without him. But he chose to stay. He chose to make a family with her, even if it meant leaving his first family. And Joon knows his desire to be with her is genuine and lasting. She feels his devotion when he presses his hands to her still-flat stomach in wonder, as he kisses her breasts and navel and pubic bone, when he lies beside her and matches his breathing to hers.

Still, even if as a wife Joon comes first, she realizes that her children will always come second. Keaka will not love or care for Joon's baby less, but the child will never be as primary in Keaka's life. If Joon has a boy, he will fail to match the memory of John-Boy. And if she gives birth to a girl, then her daughter will always be in Sarah's shadow. Joon has accepted this, and while at times she feels despair, she does not feel anger. She has chosen this, and she and her baby will bear it, and Keaka will give them all the love he can.

In January of her senior year, Sarah runs into Gordon Yu at the Kahala Mall. She is in the candy store buying a bag of hurricane popcorn—the kind with seaweed, sesame seeds, and hot Japanese crackers—when she feels a soft tap on her shoulder. She recognizes Gordon immediately. His eyes are still large and brown and a little watery, but he has grown his hair long, to his shoulders, so that the waves transform into soft curls near the end. "I remember you," he says. "Sarah Paliku."

She nods. She feels her hands start to shake and heat rise into her cheeks. The friend she's with giggles.

"What high school you at now?" he asks, casually, like they are old friends.

"Sacred Hearts," she whispers.

"The girls' school?"

She nods. He is beautiful to her still. Even behind the skinny jeans and chain belt, the affected stance that juts one hip in front of the other, the pimpled skin. With sudden clarity, she again feels the joy of walking past his house as he arrived home, the craftiness she felt when, attempting to time her appearance with that of Gordon's, she would pause to tie her shoe or tell John-Boy and Robert to hurry along. And in that rush of memories she thinks of her brother. He never teased her about Gordon, never mentioned her purposeful stride when Mrs. Yu picked up Gordon on time. John-Boy protected even the secrets no one told him.

"How you?" she asks Gordon. He describes a party he went to the night before and University of Hawai'i at Hilo, where he hopes to matriculate in the fall. Sarah tries to focus on Gordon, but she is thinking of John-Boy: his half-opened lips when he concentrated on his homework, the rough calluses on his hands from playing baseball, his easy gait when he ran bases. She is hearing the sound of the car's brakes, and the soft thump of her brother's body against the bumper. She is remembering how Mrs. Yu ran into the street.

Sarah realizes for the first time that Gordon must have waited at school for his mother for more than an hour that day. Why did he think she was late? What did she tell him when she finally arrived with John-Boy's blood on her jeans?

"What you doing now?" Gordon asks her. He flips his hair out of his eyes and playfully taps her left hip. She recognizes he is flirting. Her friend watches, smiling knowingly as John-Boy used to, and Sarah remembers what it felt like to be twelve, deep in the recesses of her first crush, and pining for Gordon with such earnestness she felt as if she were in mourning.

"I'm . . ." She pauses. What is she doing? Buying popcorn. Talking to her first crush. Remembering her brother.

John-Boy has been dead five years now, and she has marked every anniversary with private ceremonies, quietly lighting candles in her room after her mother has gone to sleep and visiting the cemetery alone, without either Grace's loud display of sobbing or Keaka's stony silence. Sarah has wound her solitude into a tight ball of grief, and now Gordon is threatening to unravel it. "I'm thinking of my brother."

Gordon glances at the ground. "Yeah, I remember him."

"Your mom was there that day."

"I know." He reaches out his hand, as if to comfort her, but Sarah doesn't take it. Still, she feels compelled to tell him what she has hidden for the past five years.

"I was thinking about you. I wasn't paying attention to the car because I was thinking about you."

"I didn't know that." Gordon turns nervously toward the counter where buckets of honey chews and red vines beckon. Sarah has assaulted him with this admission, and now she feels sorry for him. He seems so small compared to her, so young and naive. Sarah can taste salt water on her lips, and her cheeks are chilled where the air-conditioning is hitting her damp skin, and she understands that she is crying.

"It was good seeing you, I guess." Gordon edges toward the candy counter.

Sarah's friend grabs her hand and pulls her toward the door, but Sarah is rooted to the spot. Gordon changes course and makes a dash for the exit, his gait awkward in the tight jeans, and Sarah again recalls her brother's legs stretching widely as he ran. He was a beautiful runner.

She doesn't know how long she sobs next to the bins of sour gummy apples and peaches. The customers and staff move around her until at last she lets her friend lead her to the car.

Sarah is dropped off at her dad and Joon's apartment, where she spends every other weekend. Keaka is watching football with Jake, his and Joon's son. "How you?" Keaka asks as she walks through the door. He waves his hand at her without looking away from the television screen. Jake flaps a chubby arm. He's three and a half and mimics their dad's every movement.

Sarah goes to her room without speaking. She can hear the television announcer: Steelers have possession of the ball after a stunning interception. Sarah drops her purse on the floor by her bed. She turns when she hears a sound at the door. Her father is there, leaning awkwardly against the doorframe. "You okay, Princess?"

She begins to cry again. She can't help herself. She hasn't cried in front of her dad for five years, and now she is afraid of making him angry. She waits for him to yell at her to stop, but instead he pulls her to him and wraps his arms tightly around her shoulders. "Ah, baby girl," he says. "Is dis 'cause some boy?"

Sarah shakes her head. She almost wants to laugh, her father is so unaware. But then she cries even harder because her father is so unaware.

"What dis den?"

She takes a deep breath. She wants to know what she's always suspected: "Would it have been worse for you if it had been me instead of John-Boy?"

"Why you ask dis?" Keaka waits for her to reply, but when she doesn't he shakes his head. "No, it would have been da same."

Sarah knows this is the right answer, the one her father should give. The answer, in fact, that she told herself she wanted to hear. But instead of relief, she feels betrayal. She has believed for years that Keaka loved her best— more than John-Boy, more than Jake, even more than Joon. But now . . . Sarah looks into her father's face and sees that he is proud of himself. He has finally said what a good father would say, acted as a good father should act.

"What if it had been Jake?" Sarah asks, but she doesn't want an answer. Keaka's expression crumbles. Before he can speak, she interrupts him. "Or Mom? Or Joon?" Sarcasm thickens her voice. "It would have been worse for you if it was Joon."

"Why you say dat?" Keaka's tone is a warning. His face reddens, and she wonders if her dad will hit something— the wall, a mirror, the door.

But she doesn't care what he might do or how he might feel. "You would have stayed if it was Joon. You wouldn't have left us."

Keaka slams his hand against the door frame and turns his back to her. "It no be different if it was Joon. I love you all the same."

"Yea, that's the problem." Sarah's voice boils with anger. "How dare you love me the same as her."

Six months later Sarah leaves for college on the mainland. Her two oversized suitcases are filled with tank tops and jeans and heels that Keaka thinks are provocatively high but of which Grace has approved. Keaka joins his ex-wife at the airport to see their daughter off. He is reminded that this is the only child they will send to college together. Joon does not come to the airport, nor does Jake. Grace still cannot bear to see the boy, though she buys him a gift every year on his birthday.

Sarah is dry-eyed, excited. She is already thinking of her dorm and the roommates with whom she e-mails on a daily basis and will meet in six hours. She is dressed in tight jeans and two layered tank tops, a style Sarah says everyone in California is wearing. Grace cries the entire time: from the dimly lit parking garage where Keaka meets them to the ticket counter where Sarah checks her baggage to the security line, in which Grace insists on waiting with Sarah. Keaka is silent, watching his daughter. She has her mother's leanness and taut muscle structure, Grace's flat face and tall, slender nose. Keaka sees flashes of himself, though, in Sarah's broad smile and the long eyelashes she has coated with mascara. When Sarah disappears into the terminal, Grace cries even harder, and Keaka reaches out to her. Grace lets him hold her, and he lets her cry. After the years of disappointment he has caused her, he does give her this. Holding her, witnessing her sadness, is his apology.

They walk back to their cars together, and in the parking lot, they kiss each other gently on the cheek. Neither of them is much in the mood for talking. Keaka wants to get home to Joon and Jake, to forget that he already misses Sarah, to forget what it feels like to lose a child—whether to the mainland or to forever.

Back at home, Keaka opens a bottle of beer and wanders into Sarah's room. In her closet, he has kept four boxes from his days as Grace's husband. He thinks of those years like that—his days as someone else's husband.

He opens the smallest of them—he remembers, without hesitation, which one contains what he wants—and digs through the stacks of insurance documents and tax statements, copies of divorce proceedings from his lawyer, a child-sized baseball mitt whose leather has stiffened after years of sitting unused in the box, until he feels the rough curves of an ornate gold picture frame. Now, when he looks at the image, the one of him wearing a plumeria lei, he thinks not of his unhappy marriage, of his days as

Grace's husband, but of the child she was carrying when she took the photograph.

Keaka remembers when Grace hung that photograph in their sunroom. She was two days overdue and stubborn as always. When he didn't hang it at her urging, she wrestled the step stool out from the broom closet and nailed the picture to the wall herself.

He has to admit he likes the photo. He likes the faraway expression on his face. He likes that, for many years, the image pissed off his mother-in-law, who thought it shameful to have a picture of him "half naked like a native" hanging where everyone could see it. When they had family gatherings, he always made a point of showing off the photo. Only one aspect of the image bothers him: it makes him long for something he can't name.

He remembers the day Grace took the picture of him. He had wanted to go fishing with his friends, but after being out all night with Joon, it hadn't seemed right. He was feeling so bad about Joon that when Grace asked him to run to the grocery store for more raspberry jam, he bought a lei, too, from the case of flowers at the front of Safeway. Back home, Grace was sitting in the living room watching television.

He came up behind her to drape the lei over her shoulders. "Beautiful flowers for my beautiful flower," he said. She looked up at him, surprised and smiling. "I sorry I wen stay out late with da boys las' night." He sat down on the couch next to her and took her hands in his. "We start talking story and haf some beers, and ho, you know how is wit' dem. But today, I no go wit' dem. Today, I take you out. We go beach or whateva you like."

"Oh, you." She kissed him on the cheek. She forgave him easily in those days.

He made a big deal of the little trip, packing peanut butter and jelly sandwiches, bottles of water, the granola bars in green foil that she liked so much. He even took a blanket along, one of the old ones they used to keep in his car back in the days when that was the only place they could have sex, before she was pregnant, before they lived together. He didn't think Grace suspected anything about Joon, at least not then. It was all still new then.

Keaka was almost enjoying himself when Grace pulled out the camera. She always wanted him to "look natural," like smiling at a camera wasn't natural. He wanted to tell her, "People, dey smile at cameras. Das what dey do." But he kept his mouth shut.

She snapped a couple of photos and then stopped to take a bite of the sandwich he had made. He couldn't watch her eat it now that the jelly was gristled with sand. He turned his head and looked out over the water, closing his eyes slightly to see beyond the glare, and in the distance he could make out a Boston whaler bumping over the crests of the waves. He heard the camera click but kept looking over the water, wondering what else was out there he couldn't see.

THE OLD PANIOLO WAY

"Dat ting," Harrison said, reaching to touch the saddle blanket slung over Pilipo's arm. The cloth was a simple pattern, dark blue waves undulating through a turquoise sea, rough in the way wool can be. Harrison closed his eyes as he ran his fingers along its tight weave. "I wen give dat to yoa mudda when I aks her fo' marry me. She da best horsewoman I know. If yoa sista eva ride like da momma, ho. I gon hope."

Before Pili could answer him, Harrison began coughing again, hacking up blood and sputum. He deposited the pink mass as neatly as possible into a paper towel, then dropped it into the wastebasket beside his bed. Though Harrison was careful, Pili still had to take a bit of clean paper and wipe his chin. Harrison frowned impatiently, as if Pili were making a fuss over nothing, but Pili didn't want to stare at the blood even if his father wasn't bothered by it.

"Yoa momma, neva shy, her. Not like dem uddeh girls. She wen enta da Kona Stampede an' she win roping two years in a row. Ho, I proud den. Plenny men in love wit' her. Plenny like make her dere wife. But only one akamai. Only one say, I neva give you no ring. I promise fo' give you plenny horses, but. An' dat one me. Akamai yoa papa, yeah?"

"Yes, Dad," Pili said. "You were one smart man."

Harrison closed his eyes then. Pili waited for his father to say something more, but eventually the old man's wheezing became long and even, and Pili realized he had fallen asleep. Pili wondered what his father dreamt of these days, if his sleeping hours were as haunted by Mahea, Pili's mother, as his waking hours were, or if he dreamed of the girlfriends he had had after Mahea died. He had taken widowhood hard, but he had handled it in his own way.

Pili stood and adjusted the blankets, pulling them around his father's neck. Maile claimed their father didn't like to sleep with sheets touching his face, but really he didn't like the way she tucked them so tightly beneath his shoulders. Harrison had told Pili that. Actually, Harrison had said, "What, she like strangle me? I no ma-ke fast enough awready?"

Pili left his father's study and wandered to the kitchen looking for Maile. She didn't hear him at first—her back was to the kitchen door—but when he coughed to announce his presence, she turned. "Takuan?" she said, holding out a plastic container. They had been her favorite as a teen, after their mom died and later, when each of Harrison's girlfriends left him. When she divorced five years ago, Maile moved back home to be with their dad and took to eating them again in fevered spurts. Entire plastic tubs of the pickled vegetables could disappear in a single afternoon. Pili gingerly fished out one of the radishes, its exterior dyed neon yellow and the interior white as a cloud.

"How Dad?" Maile asked.

Pili knew she didn't ask because she was wondering but to fill the silence between them. She, more than anyone, understood their father's condition. She had cared for him for the past year—from the moment of his diagnosis through the radiation and chemo and through this, the end. Only in the last six weeks, when he couldn't be left alone at night, did they hire a hospice nurse for the evenings; Maile still dominated Harrison's care during the day.

"Dad was spry. He was talking to me about Mom," Pili said.

"He wheezing?"

"Not as much as last night."

"Good sign, yeah?" Maile didn't wait for Pili to answer, afraid perhaps he would disagree with her. She plucked another radish from the near-empty container and rose slowly from the chair, making her way to the wall of windows overlooking the summer pasture. The herd had been moved a couple miles away, where a deep ravine provided them some protection from the winter winds, and the field looked flat and empty without their presence.

Maile pressed her hand to the windowpane, and Pili came to stand behind her. Although she never spoke of it, he could feel the barely suppressed panic that had engulfed her since their father's diagnosis. She leaned into the cool glass as if it could steady her. Pili rested a hand on her shoulder. She was only four years older than him, but she had always treated him as a child, even through his twenties. Now he was thirty-one, an equal to her, and he hoped for once she would confide in him, that they might speak of what was to come and how they could help each other. But she was silent, and after a moment she removed her palm from the pane and shook his hand from her shoulder. "Albert is hea," she said. "Can see da dust from his car."

Outside a cloud of red rose up from the dirt road, revealing a blue Civic. Pili sighed. He would receive no confidences now. Maile walked across the kitchen to retrieve a bottle of Windex and a roll of paper towels from beneath the sink. She wiped her handprint from the glass, scrubbing until the paper shredded, and then returned the cleaning supplies to the cupboard. "Like curry tonight?"

"We had beef last night," Pili said. "I'd prefer your vegetable lasagna."

"Ah, selfish, you. I wen defrost beef dis morning. Albert, he like my curry." Maile reached into the refrigerator and pulled out a paper-wrapped package of beef. She dropped it on the cutting board, the meat's center still frozen enough for it to make a sharp clapping sound. She cubed the beef quickly, without wasting a single flick of the wrist, and the knife slid easily across the grain of the meat. Pili knew she had timed the defrosting perfectly, waiting until it was no longer frozen hard but still firm enough to cube with precision.

"Since when does someone cook for their father's nurse every night?"

"Since we lucky get such a good nurse."

"I hope you aren't trying to impress him."

Maile glared at Pili over the cutting board. He felt a small thrill of triumph, but when she looked back down, her hands trembled and he felt cruel for teasing her.

"Aloha kākou," Albert called to them from the front hall.

"In da kitchen." Maile washed her hands in the sink.

"I brought you folks some 'opihi." Albert breezed into the room, kissing Maile on the cheek and shaking Pili's hand before unpacking his duffel on the table. "My auntie picked 'em."

"Where?"

"You know I no can tell you." He winked at Maile. 'Opihi harvesting was forbidden since the colonies had been overfished, but certain families still knew where to find the tasty limpets.

Maile laughed, her voice trilling at the top note, and for the thousandth time in the week since Pili had returned home, he wondered if his sister was in love with Albert. She often flirted with him, but she did so gently, as one might a favorite friend or a surrogate sibling, a brother who was actually around when she needed him.

Albert breathed deeply. "Smells 'ono in here." He patted Maile gently on the arm, then picked up his duffel and left for the study. "Aloha, Uncle." Albert's voice echoed through the house, and Pili heard his father grunt sleepily in response. A few minutes later the toilet flushed, which meant Albert had emptied Harrison's catheter. Next Albert would sponge Harrison's chest and underarms, then rub lotion into his hands and feet. Albert had a set routine, an order for his duties, and Pili had memorized it. He could imagine Albert moving through each task, his body curving around the hospital bed and chair like water curves around rocks.

In the kitchen, Maile rinsed rice in a colander. She ran her fingers through the translucent kernels, feeling for rotten grains and the occasional rock shard, and when she was satisfied the rice was clean, she poured it into the cooker and added water. She moved without thinking, without grace or artistry, and watching her, Pili was suddenly gripped by disappointment. He wished his sister were extravagant in her movements and emotions, in her treatment of him and their father. Instead, the most pas-

sion she could muster was for her pickled radishes and a
smudged windowpane.

Pili left the kitchen to hover in the doorway of his
father's study. Albert had wrapped a hot cloth around
Harrison's face. Now he lifted it away and slathered shaving cream on Harrison's skin. Harrison pressed his lips
together in a tight smile, and Albert began to shave his
face, starting with the left sideburn and working his way
down to the chin.

"You've got a steady hand," Pili called from the doorway. Albert smiled and motioned for Pili to join them.

"No distract 'im," Harrison said to Pili. "He get one
razor at my neck. I no can escape."

"If you like talk when I shave you, you no more have
no lips."

"Auwē! Look, son, he like t'reaten me. I glad you hea
fo' see dis." Both Albert and Harrison laughed. After a
moment Pili joined in, but he had the feeling this was a
practiced joke between them and he merely an accidental
audience.

Albert touched Harrison's face firmly, lifting the skin
at his jaw to get a good, clean shave on the neck, and then,
when the shaving was finished, wiping down Harrison's
face with a cool cloth and patting his skin with Old Spice.
Pili was jealous. He wanted his father to laugh with him
as he did with Albert. He wanted Albert to touch him
as Albert touched Harrison. Pili wanted to be either of
them, or both.

"After this shave, you like go holoholo?" Albert teased.

"I'll go get your good boots," Pili added. "Make sure they're shined."

"Like find me some good-lookin' woman fo' dance," Harrison said. He lifted his arms and held them curved around the air in front of him, like he was holding a woman around the waist. "Hell, like find one māhū if he haf da kine legs and know how fo' two-step." He laughed hard at that, and Albert with him, but this time Pili remained silent.

The subject of māhūs always left Pili reeling. Sometimes he felt his father was purposefully aiming jokes at him, and other times he believed Harrison was just a product of his generation and place. The debate over his father's intentions had plagued Pili since he was twelve and had accompanied his father to O'ahu. Pili had, until that trip, assumed his father knew everything about him, and that between them no secrets existed.

They had flown to O'ahu so Harrison could finalize the arrangements for the sale of two ponies to a polo player on North Shore. Pili went along to witness the inspection of the horses, the negotiations, and the gentlemanly airs of the polo men. Selling to them was different than selling to a fellow paniolo.

After the papers were signed, Harrison drove to his sister's place in Kailua, and in the evening the three of

them—Harrison, Pili, and Pili's aunt Inez—visited
Waikīkī. They strolled along Kalākaua Avenue to take ad-
vantage of the view of the beach. The waves were small,
hardly the kind of thundering mountains Pili had seen on
North Shore that morning, but he barely noticed. The
few times they had come to O'ahu, they had never visited
Waikīkī. Now Pili was there, with his father and aunt,
having been chosen over his sister, and he felt very grown
up and important. He would have liked if his mother had
been along too, but she had stayed behind to continue
training the two-year-olds and a pair of five-year-old stallions she had taken on from another ranch. Later, when
Pili reflected back on this trip, he would realize it had oc-
curred just a couple months before his mother's accident.

In Waikīkī, at the International Marketplace, Pili pe-
rused the vendors' stalls, studying the coconut purses
and overpriced shell combs lining the tables. He stepped
into the T-shirt shops to feel the air-conditioning chill
the sweat on his face and arms, and he stared through the
windows of the bathing suit stores with their bikinis and
pareos in bright flower patterns. Outside the Moana Surfrider, Pili paused to watch the bellhops as they jumped
to open car doors and load luggage on carts made from
gleaming brass. The young men were dressed smartly in
white coats with matching white gloves to keep the brass
from being smudged. They moved with grace, their bodies bending and twisting to lift Samsonite suitcases and to
open doors and to prance with their carts into the hotel.

Pili watched them as he might a parade of young fillies, captivated by their energy and beauty.

Harrison led them past the Royal Hawaiian Shopping Center, which was poorly lit and dank and curved in endless hallways. Inez asked to look at more stores, but Harrison laughed at her for acting like a tourist and they went instead to walk around the grounds of the Royal Hawaiian. The hotel was the pink of a wilted lokelani flower. Pili stared at its high walls and felt that the small, square windows were fifty pairs of eyes returning his gaze.

The bellhops at the Royal Hawaiian were dressed just as well as those at the Moana, but their movements were heavier, less lithe, stiffer. They, too, wore crisp jackets, but in black rather than white, and this, combined with their movements, made them seem older. They were not as smooth-cheeked either. In fact, one bellhop even had the fuzz of a young mustache. Pili watched him the most closely. He was probably in his early twenties, with full lips, brown hair bleached to red from the sun, and fine lines at the outer corners of his eyes. He had a weathered look about him, like a sailor, and Pili wondered if the man's skin would feel rough or smooth to the touch.

Harrison and Inez walked with their heads bent together, his arm tucked around her waist. Harrison was describing Mahea's latest feat, breaking one of the five-year-old stallions. The horses had belonged to another rancher, and only Mahea would take them on. They weren't worth any of the other paniolos' time. But Mahea

loved working with horses like these, taming and calm-
ing them, creating a bond where none had existed before.
Harrison's descriptions focused on Mahea's more daring tactics—Pili knew his father loved impressing other
women with stories of Mahea—and when Inez gasped in
both fear and admiration, Harrison smiled broadly.

However, Pili didn't love these stories. They left him
dry-mouthed and jumpy. He tried to ignore his father,
turning to look again at the rough-cheeked bellhop, and
this time the young man noticed and smiled. Pili felt his
throat close. All he could think to do was run, but when
he caught up to his father and aunt, he immediately wished
he hadn't fled.

They returned along Kūhiō Avenue, which was grit-
tier and dirtier than Kalākaua, with more bars and men
in military costume. Pili paused to stare at the front window of a bar, its glass shattered in a cobweb pattern, its
fragmented pieces held together with black duct tape, and
when he looked back toward the street, he saw his father
and aunt had again walked ahead of him. They stopped
when the light turned red at Lewers, and Pili dodged two
Japanese women with shopping bags in order to catch up.
At the corner, he found himself pressed into the crowd,
standing beside a tall woman in a black evening gown.
Her legs were long and shapely, covered in mesh stockings
that drew attention to a deep slit in the dress revealing her
left thigh. She had black hair, as black as her dress, hair
that was dyed over and over until it was stiff and dry. Her

lips were plush, like the lips of the bellhop Pili had admired, and her eyelashes were thickly layered. Pili stared at her without meaning to.

She smiled. "Good evening, sir." Her voice was like cigarette smoke curling in the evening air.

"Good evening, Auntie," Pili answered, smiling back at her.

She laughed, clearly delighted, but where Pili had expected the high, floating laugh of his mother, this woman's laughter dropped low and hovered.

Harrison noticed Pili then. Immediately he tensed, and Pili could tell something had upset him. Harrison nodded politely at the woman and took Pili's hand, though Pili was far too old to hold hands. When the light turned, Harrison marched them across the street.

Inez had to run to catch up. "Oh, Harrison," she said, laughing, and rested her hand on his arm. "So country, you." But Harrison was not laughing, and Pili wondered what had made him so serious.

"Boy, you see anyting diff'rent 'bout dat woman? Da one you call Auntie?" Harrison demanded when they reached the other street corner.

Pili shook his head.

"Nutting?" Inez asked more gently, a smile prying at her lips.

"She wen dye 'er hair?"

Inez laughed. "Yeah, she wen dye 'er hair. Dat not da only ting she wen do."

"Dat one māhū, son," Harrison said finally. "A man like tink he one woman."

Pili knew what a māhū was, though he had never seen one in person, only on television or in movies. But there was a boy in school—Jesse—who everyone said was māhū. In grade school he used to chase Pili and his friends around the playground, chase them like the girls did, and sometimes he'd catch them and pin them to the ground, sitting on them so his stuff was almost touching theirs. He moved like a girl, he dressed like a girl wearing pants. He even had the skin of a girl, clear and smooth. Pili had little interest in Jesse other than to copy his math homework, but he made fun of him anyway along with the other boys.

Inez led them back to the parking lot where they had left the car. "Funny, yeah, Dad," Pili said, as Harrison fit the key into its lock. "Māhūs, dey try so hard fo' look good, but dey neva beautiful like da real ting."

Pili watched his father's shoulders relax. Harrison smiled. "Dat, Son, is da trut'. Nutting beautiful like one real woman."

In bed that night Pili thought of the bellhop, the one at the Royal Hawaiian. I am not māhū, he said to himself. He did not want to play as if he were a girl, nor dress like a woman, nor powder his face as his aunt did. But he did think about touching a man in the way his friends spoke of touching a woman. He wanted to feel the soft hairs on another man's arm, and press his hand against the smooth landscape of another man's chest. He wanted to stand so close to a man, he could breathe him in, and instead of a girl's passionfruit chapstick or coconut lotion, he would smell musk and heat and that peculiar sour of dried sweat.

I am not māhū, Pili repeated to himself. Yet, when he had told Harrison nothing was as beautiful as the real thing, he had not meant women but men.

Albert refused to join Maile and Pili for dinner in the evening. Maile often asked him to, but he always declined, and eventually she would relent and promise to set aside a plate of food for whenever he got hungry. Pili never caught Albert eating—Pili never saw him do anything except care for or talk to Harrison—but each morning the food had disappeared, and the plate was washed and dried and back in the cupboard.

While Pili and Maile ate, Albert sat beside Harrison, the bedside lamp casting a yellow circle around the two of them. They spoke off and on. Harrison liked when Albert read aloud from *West Hawai'i Today* or a breeding bull catalog or, more rarely, the Hawaiian prayer book that had belonged to Mahea. Eventually Harrison drifted off. Sometimes he slept through half the night, but usually he was wracked by violent coughing fits that were calmed only when Albert administered codeine or, increasingly, morphine.

Pili spied on Albert and his father. He wasn't proud of this, but he did it anyway. In the evening, on his way to the bathroom, to his bedroom, to select a book from the shelf in the hall, he'd glance into the study to see what they were doing or saying or even how Albert's body was positioned in relation to Harrison's. Again, in the early morning, when Pili awoke to conference with his assistant in San Francisco, he'd peek in on Harrison and Albert, and they'd still be together, side by side, just as Pili had left them the night before. Once Pili even glimpsed Albert leaning over Harrison's body and dabbing gently at his temples where a layer of perspiration shone. Pili wondered what made Albert care for Harrison like that. What made him so selfless? And how could he be so comfortable with Harrison? At night, in bed, Pili wondered if his father favored Albert, or even Maile, over Pili. Did he crave their care more than the paltry conversation Pili offered? Was Pili perhaps even a joke among them—they who knew each other's habits so well?

One night, plagued by these doubts and unable to sleep, Pili made his way to the kitchen. As he passed his father's study, he peeked beneath the door, but no light seeped from the room and he wondered if, during the long hours of the night, Albert read by flashlight or slept in the chair beside Harrison's bed or merely sat in the dark with his own thoughts and Harrison's haggard breath to keep him company. In the kitchen, Pili didn't bother to turn on the lights. He poured himself a glass of water and walked to the window where just a few days before Maile had pressed her hand to the pane. The land appeared black and thick as a wool rug, and the sky was dotted with tiny pinpricks of stars. He felt impossibly small.

"It's dark in here," a voice said. Pili turned to see Albert leaning against the kitchen door frame, one hand wrapped around the wood and the other resting on his thigh. "Do you always stand around in the dark?"

"I can see the stars better with the lights off."

"In that case, I'll let my eyes adjust." Albert found his dinner plate and heated it in the microwave. He sat at the table and motioned for Pili to do the same. The room was warm still from the sun beating into it all day, and along the bottom edge of the window frame condensation had gathered in large, drooping pearls. Pili wanted to dip his finger into those droplets and see if he could taste the night air.

"How you holding up?" Albert asked. He had rice in his mouth, and the smell of beef stew was strong.

"Fine, I guess." Pili shrugged.

"You getting along okay during the day?"

"Sure. My sister runs a one-woman show, and my father and I are merely the audience. A very well-fed audience."

"I'll tell you a secret." Albert leaned toward Pili. "I've gained six pounds in the two months I've worked here!" He took another bite of stew and chewed it sideways, like a cow, his jaw working in a left to right motion. "But I can't complain. I've never had a placement where I was fed like this. Your sister knows how to take care of a man. I just wish she would relax a little. I would give up the dinners to see her chill out."

"I've been trying to get her to relax since we were kids."

Albert laughed as if Pili were making a joke.

"I'd like to help her during the day," Pili said, "but I don't know what to do and she won't show me. I end up just sitting and talking with Dad most of the time."

"Nothing wrong with that."

"But she's doing all the work. I feel like a schlump."

"Don't. It's her choice. I think it's great you sit and talk with your dad." Pili watched as a carrot bounced from one side of Albert's tongue to the other. "I'll tell you something: I was seventeen when my grandmother died. I was her hānai son. She had raised me since I was four, made me her own, but she was old when I came along, you know? I cared for her at the end. It's what made me become a nurse. But being her caretaker was a full-time job, and I don't mean time. I mean, when I became her caretaker, I ceased to be her grandson. I had to know every part of her body. I had to see her in ways a child should never see a parent. And I didn't mind. I loved her too much to mind. But for her? How humiliating. For her grandson to stare on her naked body, to wipe her mouth and her 'ōkole, to tend to bedsores and see and touch every part of her skin. To empty her catheter and clean her feeding tube and wash out her mouth at night with a washcloth because her face had shrunk and her dentures no longer fit her mouth and a toothbrush was too rough on her gums." He stood and made his way to the sink. "You don't want to be a nurse to your father, and you don't have to be. I wish your sister would realize that, too."

Albert poured himself a glass of water and gazed into it. For a moment, he had a look of vulnerability, a boy lost in his thoughts. Then he lifted the glass to his lips and gulped down the water, and the briskness of his movement undid the brief impression of youth. Albert washed his dishes and dried them neatly. When he was finished, he leaned awkwardly against the counter. "I guess I just wanted to say . . ." He opened his mouth and closed it again. "I mean, I didn't want to unload that, but . . ." He glanced down at his hands and then looked up. "You should know your father's swelling in the face continues to be severe in the morning. I'm going to raise his bed to forty degrees and see if that helps."

Albert swept out of the room as silently as he had entered. Pili heard him open the door to the study and close it again. The stars were higher in the sky now, and brighter, and Pili remained in the kitchen for a while longer wondering if Albert spoke to Maile with such candor.

Pili and Albert's brief conversation seemed to shift the wall that had previously stood between them. Whereas before Pili had wandered to his room after dinner to work or read, now he joined Albert in Harrison's study. Pili discovered, to his relief, that with Albert present the study felt less claustrophobic than when Pili was alone with his father, and Harrison seemed more at ease, too. With an audience, Harrison spoke at greater length and with fewer pauses, and he seemed less susceptible to the pain in his arms and legs. Pili began to think company served as a kind of opiate for him.

Maile joined them one evening, and she wore her hair loose around her shoulders. She looked pretty, more serene. She spoke of the riding lessons she gave, and when the subject was broached of how she and Pili had learned to ride, they laughed together and pointed at their father. "Dad put Maile on a sweet old mare, and I was given a stud colt. That's how he taught us," Pili said.

"Bulai, you," Harrison laughed. "He no stay on one toy horse if I go glue 'im dere."

"Dad's right," Maile chimed in. "Pili neva have no balance when he one keiki."

"In my defense, I had a bad ear infection as a baby, and it affected my balance for most of my childhood."

"Ah, da momma say dat. Pili jus' no can ride. I tell you da trut', but. He take good care da horses. Mo betta dan da sista. Maile, she like ride 'em but neva like train 'em. Das da hard part, yeah. Pili, he stay wit' dem fo' long time. He wen clean 'em, curry dem, brush 'em. He like be da firs' get 'em unda da saddle. Dem horses, dey get so dey need fo' see him evry day. If Pili stay friend house one night, da horses get restless. Dey know he left 'em. Dey get like dat, you know. Dey get so dey need fo' be wit' da one take care dem."

"I took plenny care da horses, Dad," Maile said.

"Nutting much go wata dem, hay dem. Your brudda, he neva haf no balance. He know how fo' be wit' dem, but. Mo bettah dan anybody, him."

Maile didn't answer, but Pili knew she wanted to. He could see it in the way she worked her jaw. Albert must have sensed it, too. He asked Maile about her students, helped the conversation shift, and by the end of the evening they were all laughing again.

When Pili was a boy, he often followed his father to the porch in the evening, where Harrison liked to sit and drink and take stock of the day. The nights always started the same. Pili would watch his father flip open the top of a cigarette box and draw out a cigarette with his lips like a horse taking an apple from a man's hand. Harrison smoked slowly, with evident pleasure, and Pili knew not to speak but to wait for his father to settle into himself and the night and whatever conversation Harrison wished to have. As an adult, Pili would credit the patience he learned on these evenings for his ability to build his own marketing firm and to stick it out through the lean early years before success arrived.

Pili remembered how the wood porch remained warm from the day's heat and the air smelled of dried grass, cow dung, and sweat, both the pungent animal sweat of the horses and Harrison's sweat, like sulfur and pine sap and dust. Harrison drank his beer in long, silent pulls, and when he bent back his head to catch the final dregs, his Adam's apple jiggled. After the first beer was finished, Harrison would lean back and sigh, "Ah, hit da spot."

As the light bled from the sky, Harrison became a watery outline, a shadow, and if no one put on the porch light, he eventually disappeared from view altogether. This dissipation scared and thrilled Pili, for to lose sight of his father was to be closer to him, to feel rather than see him. Finally, when Pili could barely stand the silence any longer, Harrison spoke, and he talked the way he rode, with the quiet, steady rhythm of a man at ease.

Harrison always started by describing the work he had done that day and what was still to be done the next. He detailed which horses needed to be shod and which might soon be sold, and he told stories about the paniolos and the herd. He also solicited Pili's advice, asking if his son thought the makai stretch of the bull paddock needed repair or if they had enough hay stored for the winter months, and these questions were what Pili waited for.

On the porch, Pili had Harrison to himself. He didn't have to share his father with the other paniolos. Harrison wasn't distracted by the cattle or his horses, and neither Mahea nor Maile were there to interrupt with their opinions. Harrison belonged completely to Pili, and he spoke to him as one man to another. Pili gave careful thought to all his father's questions, sometimes even waiting to answer them until the following evening. And on the rare occasion neither Harrison nor Pili had anything to say, they sat in companionable silence, each with his own thoughts, and shared their solitude and the evening.

Pili tried to remember when those evenings had ended, the intimacy faded away. When could he no longer speak to his father? Or had his father stopped knowing how to speak to him? Sometime in his early teens, Pili believed, around the time of their visit to Waikīkī, or just after, when Pili's mother died.

Now, as his father was dying, Pili was haunted by the desire to re-create the intimacy he and Harrison had once shared. Pili wondered what might bring them back to that kind of closeness, and he began to think that if he could just come out to his dad—and Maile, too—then perhaps he would regain the relationships he missed. In San Francisco, his coming out—along with the honesty and self-realization that it required of him—was cheered and celebrated among his friends, and championed without hesitation. But in Hawai'i, Pili was unsure of his desires and of himself.

Here, Pili felt as if he were a child still: doubtful, unwhole, his being as solid as vapor. On the mainland Pili knew who he was: successful marketing magnate, occasional club favorite, excellent dinner companion. On island he was none of those. He was reduced to simply being his father's son. He had remained hidden from his father and sister, separated by an ocean and twelve years of living on the mainland. He had carefully crafted his semiannual visits to coincide with the arrival of aunts and uncles so he would never be alone with Harrison or Maile, and though he offered to pay for them to fly to San Francisco, he knew they wouldn't accept. They had the ranch to run. Now Pili regretted these decisions and wished he had more ground to stand on, more recent history with them.

A warm spell came, and in the evenings, after Harrison had fallen asleep, Albert and Pili would sit in the hot study and sweat. On the third evening of this, Pili suggested they have a beer on the porch. "We won't be long—just enough to cool off a little." Albert hesitated at first, but once outside, he released a long sigh of relief. The wind swept down the mountain breathlessly and cooled their damp skin. The sky was lavender, delicate and high, and in the distance, the unfinished skeletons of homes being constructed were black silhouettes. "Don't you miss being here?" Albert asked.

"Of course. How could I not?" Pili held out his arms as if he might fold the landscape into them. "I love the horses. I love those mountains and the ocean. I love my family. I just also happen to love California." Pili took a sip of his beer. "What about you? Are you happy here?"

"I like the islands enough."

"Enough? That's not a ringing endorsement. Where else would you like to live?"

"Seattle maybe. Or San Diego. Somewhere big but not too big. I hear nurses are needed everywhere. I could find a job easily."

"Why stay then?"

"My family."

"Do they need you? I mean, are you taking care of one of them?"

"No, they're all healthy, and they don't need my money, though I spoil my baby cousins. But they're my family, so I stay. Isn't that why you're here?"

"I'm just here because my dad is dying," Pili said drily.

"I don't believe that's the only reason. You're here because you love him, you cherish the time you have with him. It's not about him dying but about the two of you being together." Albert tilted his head and pressed together his lips. His expression gave him an air of certainty. Pili didn't dare disagree, but he wondered if Albert was right. Had Pili come and stayed when his father was diagnosed? Or when he went through chemo? No, he had flown in five months ago for a four-day weekend and then out again, and his father, sick with the protocol, had barely been awake for Pili's visit. Pili knew Albert's vision of him was suspect, but he nodded anyway, as if it were true, and Albert smiled with satisfaction.

In another place and time, Pili would have asked Albert to dinner in some quiet Italian restaurant or for drinks at one of those cozy seafood places on the Bay. After dinner they'd walk to a hotel or Pili's apartment and they'd find what they were seeking in each other. Albert would be a rudder for Pili, the better part of his conscience, and for Albert, Pili would be—what? Sails? Inspiration to move, to see new places and people, to embrace a life away from these tiny islands?

Albert coughed and Pili's fantasies drained away, but they left behind a residue of hope and nervousness. He finished his beer. The snow on Mauna Kea shimmered in the moonlight, and the air was so clean and thin the mountain appeared closer than it actually was, so close Pili thought he might skim his fingers along its icy peaks. He glanced over at Albert. "Why don't you speak pidgin all the time?"

"My grandmother taught English at the high school, so she was real strict about how us kids talked. With your dad and Maile it's different. It feels natural."

"Funny, I never speak it anymore. I had to relearn how to talk when I went to college, and I never went back."

"The mainland that bad?"

Pili laughed. "No, not so bad. But for me . . . Pidgin was just one more way I was different, you know?"

Albert nodded. He brought his hands to his lap and stared at them for a moment, and then, quietly, he asked, "Are you out?"

So he knows, Pili thought. "Not to my family. Are you . . . ?"

"My family doesn't know either."

"How do you keep things quiet?"

"Honolulu." Albert rubbed his hand against his cheek. "I'm inconspicuous enough there, you know? The coconut wireless doesn't stretch from O'ahu to Big Island."

"I'd still feel suffocated if I were you."

"It's better us feeling that way maybe," Albert said. "Better than them knowing and feeling hurt or disappointed."

"I think I'd rather risk my dad's disappointment than have him die and leave me to regret the distance between us." As Pili said this, he knew it to be true.

"Just because you feel regret doesn't mean he does. He's thinking everything is fine, and you're convinced there's a distance."

"Because there is." Pili threw his hands up.

"For you but not for him." Albert tapped his finger against Pili's chest. "Coming out is only about *you* feeling good."

Pili pushed Albert's finger away. "This isn't just about me."

"Then who else?"

"It's about family dynamics."

"Your dad is dying. Those are the family dynamics."

"You know nothing about our family dynamics." Pili heard his voice rising but didn't stop it. "It's not like you have the balls to tell—"

"Pili!" Maile had her face pressed to the screen door, her voice strained and high. "Whas dat language fo'?"

Pili and Albert froze, staring at each other, waiting to hear what the other might say. Pili wondered how much of their conversation Maile had overheard. He scrambled for some explanation, but the silence stretched long and taut. Finally, Albert cleared his throat. "Sorry, Maile. We just got worked up about politics." He looked pointedly at Pili, and Pili understood, but if Albert thought he was protecting her by his secrecy, Pili knew better. Albert's silence had allowed Maile's crush to flourish, and Pili was sure Albert's concealment would eventually hurt her. Either Maile would think Albert's lack of reciprocity was her fault, or she'd feel betrayed.

Pili was frustrated. He wanted everything out in the open. He wanted to unburden himself. He wanted to tell Maile to stop cooking elaborate meals, to find a different man, to find a different kind of man. Pili felt a hard nugget of purpose forming in his stomach. Maile came to stand behind Albert, the screen door slapping gently against its frame. Pili would tell her everything right now. He would tell her about himself, about Albert. He didn't owe Albert anything.

Maile rested her hand on Albert's shoulder. She was wearing a purple tank top and a pair of silk shorts. Her hair was mussed; sleep clung to her eyelashes. Albert watched Pili, waiting for him to say something, but Pili's determination evaporated. Maile looked so gentle, surprisingly feminine, just like their mother in her nightclothes, and Pili had no words.

There's always tomorrow, he thought. Tomorrow he'd tell her everything. "Sorry, Mai. We were being kāne. We'll keep it down now." Pili forced a laugh.

"Kāne, my ass. Keiki more like it." This time the screen door slammed behind her.

"Thanks for the chat," Pili mumbled to Albert. He rose and followed his sister into the house. He was angry with Albert and disappointed in himself. In his bedroom, Pili stripped and turned off the light. Tomorrow.

By the time Pili awoke the next morning, Maile had taken off to town for a hair appointment. He had slept well and deeply. He no longer felt as defensive as he had the night before, but he was reluctant to face Albert all the same.

Maile had left Pili a note to fix one of the hayracks, so as soon as he had dressed, Pili headed down to the outside paddocks. The fix was easy. The grill and rack had separated, so Pili cut a bit of plastic tubing to make a sleeve and hold the two pieces together perfectly. While he was with the horses, he took the time to brush them and check their teeth and hooves. They were in good shape, and their shared lot was immaculate. Maile must have raked before leaving for her appointment. Pili shook his head at her. He went into the barn and carried a bale out to the lot, taking the time to spread part of the hay across the ground and then leaving the rest in the corner for the horses to eat. Pili knew his sister would hate seeing such a mess, but he was convinced the horses were more comfortable this way. If left to their own habits, they would spread excess hay across the entire lot.

In a neighboring paddock the old paniolos, Keo and Joe, kept their horses. These animals fed from the ground, no racks in sight. Harrison had always said horses were meant to eat from the ground. He didn't trust racks and hay nets because of the unnatural angle they forced on a feeding animal. Keo and Joe obviously kept to this wisdom. Harrison had taught them everything they knew, and they weren't likely to go against him. But Maile was eager to embrace another way. Did she honestly believe the racks were better, or were they her way of making her own mark on the ranch operations?

Pili reached a hand out to a red roan, one of Joe's, and the animal nuzzled his jeans pocket, looking for a treat. He didn't have any, but he rubbed the mare's chin, and its ears tilted forward. The horses were well groomed and happy, their eyes bright, their coats glossy. They appeared no different from Maile's, but Pili wondered if they felt different, if Joe and Keo's horses might be a little happier, a little freer. He wanted to know what Keo and Joe thought of Maile's way with the animals, and what she thought of theirs.

Pili made his way into the barn, poking his head into the unused stalls and the tack room, which looked much the same as in his childhood. His father's office, though, was barely recognizable. Once it had been the hub of the ranch. Ledgers and calendars had covered the desk, with Harrison's appointments marked in red ink and notes on the herds penciled in the margins. Hawaiian hymns crackled from a record player, and over that the telephone was always ringing. Now the office had the hushed air of a museum. These days it stored awards, boxes of receipts held on to for ages, old bills long ago paid and filed, Harrison's two favorite saddles, and a collection of decorated blinders he kept on hand for parades. An old hackamore, the leather stained black from sweat and twisted and falling apart, was abandoned on the planks that had once served as his desk.

Pili climbed the ladder to the hayloft. When he was a boy, he could scramble up and down the rungs with his eyes closed and a saddle blanket in each arm. Now he took the steps carefully, testing one and then the next, clinging to the railings tightly. He wished he could remember when he started to be fearful, when he learned to respect falling, pain, death.

In the loft, Pili lay back on the hay. Below him, the horses moved in their stalls and he remembered the joy he had felt when he came here as a boy. He breathed deeply, but the dust caught in his throat and made him cough. He laughed at himself. The loft had been more romantic when he was a child. He hadn't seen its drawbacks when he was ten.

Back then, Harrison had collected saddle blankets, which he stored in the barn office. Harrison used a couple of them, but the rest rose in precarious piles, spilling over his paperwork, breeding certificates and bills. He claimed the blankets were part of his filing system. After Pili's mother died, Harrison kept her blankets there, too, and Pili would often steal the one with the blue waves and carry it up to the hayloft and cover the hay.

For Pili, that blanket was a flying carpet or a sled in mountain snow or an energy field ready to teleport him to anywhere he could dream of going. The cloth held magic—the brilliant dyes, the thick weave, the tiny, soft tufts of wool coming off it as it aged. Other times, typically at the end of winter when the hay was low, Pili would climb into the rafters above the loft and jump with the blanket tucked beneath his feet, surfing the air for those few thrilling seconds of freefall before he landed with a muted thump, a puff of grass-scented dust rising around him. Harrison used to get after him for thumping around in the hayloft, but he never got really angry about it, and Pili came to understand that his game was a secret between them, a tacit allowance on Harrison's part in an otherwise strict and rigorous childhood.

Pili wished he could clamber up to those rafters again, but the hay was too low and he no longer had a boy's casual confidence with heights. He hadn't realized how much he missed the barn. He missed the way it felt heavy and sturdy in the wind, he missed the smell of the horses, their droppings and the honeyed perfume of dried hay. Only now the barn felt like a shell. The person who once filled it, who had made it move and live, was slowly leaving. The horses and the bustle of the paniolos and the mountains of hay still lived in this place, but Harrison did not.

When Pili returned to the house, he was surprised to find Albert in the kitchen pulling a plate of food from the microwave. "You're here early," Pili said coolly, not forgetting their previous tension.

"I wanted to come early to see you. I'm sorry about how last night went." Albert held the hot plate of food between them. "He's your father, and I'm his nurse."

Pili stood in the doorway.

"You know how I feel, but you will do what you will do."

"That's true." Pili followed him into the study.

When Harrison saw them, he immediately protested the plate of food, claiming he wasn't hungry. "You need this, Uncle," Albert said firmly. "I know better than you." He held the spoon in front of Harrison's mouth, waiting with a patience that brooked no disagreement, and eventually Harrison relented and parted his lips.

Pili wondered if Albert knew better than him, too. After all, Pili wished for a rudder. Maybe Albert had given it to him.

He felt himself soften. When Harrison finally finished eating, Pili said: "Dad, what if I took Albert down to see the herd tomorrow?" He turned to Albert. "I mean, if you don't mind driving up here on your day off."

Albert shrugged, but Pili could tell he was pleased.

"Good tinking, son," Harrison said. "And while stay, cut some kiawe wood fo' give Keo."

"What he like use it for?" Albert asked.

"He like burn fo' smoke da meat. Wen' hunting, him. Get one wild boar he like cook."

"I like eat some!" Albert laughed.

Before they could speak any more of the trip, they heard the front door open and Maile's voice came floating to them. "Eh, Pili? Dad? I home. Bettah not be napping you two."

She appeared in the doorway. "Albert! You come early today." She tossed her hair. "Nice, yeah?" She had dyed it a deep brick red, and styled it into a gigantic wave around her head that reminded Pili of Annette Cardona in the movie *Grease*.

"Beautiful," Albert said, smiling. Pili nodded.

"Like one red hibiscus," Harrison said.

"Tanks, Dad."

"Ah, but. Tink I hea da flower calling. She like get 'er color back. Look mo bettah on her." Harrison laughed, and then turned to Albert. "What else you like do when Pili come fo' take you see da herd? Mebbe go down Joe place fo' see da new foal?"

Maile looked stricken, then heartbroken, then livid. Pili watched the emotions like they were on a film reel, one leading into the next, finishing with a tight smile. She lifted her chin slightly and left for her room.

Albert had noticed her reaction too. He glanced sidelong

at Pili. If Albert hadn't looked at him like that, Pili might have ignored Maile's departure, but now he had to check on her. Without speaking, he slipped from the study. He stood in front of Maile's closed door for a moment and then knocked softly. "What?" she called through the wall.

When he opened the door, she was seated at her desk, Harrison's ledgers spread in front of her. She was filling them in for him. Later, she would take them to him to look over and approve.

"I was just checking you were alright."

"What, I nomo look awright?"

"No, you look great. I just thought . . . you know how Dad can be."

"What you mean?" She used that high-pitched voice that told Pili she knew exactly what he meant but wasn't going to admit it.

"Him teasing you like that, about your hair."

"I used to it by now." She looked down at the ledgers again.

"You don't have to take that from him. Really, it was too much."

"It's not important. You know how he get wit' me."

"I wish you wouldn't let him."

She studied Pili. "Ah, it's better dis way," she sighed. "It's better me dan you, eh?"

"What does that mean?"

"Nutting." She shook her head as if to banish a thought. "You really gon take Albert fo' see da herd?"

"Tomorrow some time."

"I jus' no can believe . . . I say plenny times I like take 'im, and now he goes wit' you.

"I said let's go tomorrow, and he said sure."

"But *I* said I like . . ." Her voice trailed off.

Pili could guess how Maile's invitation had played out: She had mentioned taking Albert to see the herd, a half dozen times probably, but without any clear intentions. She had never set a date, never arranged to leave her duties at the ranch, never asked Albert which days might work for him. Albert, aware he was merely the nurse, hadn't pressed the issue. And now Maile was angry at Pili for making the trip happen. He took a deep breath. "How about we go together then?" He tried to sound genuinely enthused by the idea.

Maile stared at Pili through her thick eyelashes, a withering look she had perfected as a teenager. "Den who can take care of Dad? Tink, Pili. Fo' jus' one second, tink."

"What do you want then? Do you want me to stay with Dad and you can take Albert out? I'll do it if you want me to."

She sighed heavily. "No, take Albert. It's fine." She used a tone of voice that said it wasn't.

"Maile. I'd like to make it okay."

"And you no know?" Maile threw her hands up in the air.

"Do you have feelings for Albert? Is that it?"

"Auwē, you neva get it." Her voice dripped with condescension.

"For goodness sakes! You're not getting anywhere with Albert, you know. He's not straight." Pili crossed his arms over his chest and waited for her response.

She remained silent, staring at him, and when she finally spoke she did so very quietly. "You tink I no know dat? Us friends, remember? Good friends. Best friends."

Pili let his arms fall to his sides. "I didn't realize . . ." He felt embarrassed, as if he'd been scolded. He had deeply misjudged his sister, and Albert, too. Apparently Maile was more understanding than Pili gave her credit for, and Albert's secretiveness the previous night had been about protecting Pili, not himself.

"He is my only friend dese days." Maile spoke slowly, with a sense of regret. "He is da only person I like talk to. Da only one I tell tings to. Since Dad got sick, you tink I can go drive, go fo' visit Kona, or fo' see my old friends in Hilo? No way! Even in Waimea, da women I know no like come sit hea, do nutting, jus' whisper and Dad in da uddeh room dying. But, you know, I neva worry 'cause I have Albert. And den you come." She paused to look at Pili, and when she spoke again, her words came faster and louder. "Suddenly you like talk story wit' him and you like be wit' him, and what about me? All da time, you-him-Dad, and I jus' some woman who cook fo' da tree of you. Das all you care about. When I make da next meal."

"You know it's not like that," Pili pleaded. "We loved when you joined us that one evening. I wish you would sit with us more often."

She puffed air through her nose, a sound of disbelief.

"Really, Maile. I like when you're there." Pili stopped. He wanted to say more, to tell her more, as he'd promised himself he would do. But first, he had to soften her. "I'll make this thing with Albert up to you. I'll make dinner for all of us on Sunday and we'll sit and eat with Dad, okay? And on Monday you take a day and go to Kona and I'll stay with Dad and you can have some time to be with friends." He waited for her to respond.

"You really like make it right?" She crossed her arms over her chest, but her expression was soft, ready to forgive.

"Yes. Really."

She sighed again. "I guess dat hastu be enough."

"And Maile, there's something else." Pili looked down at the ground and took a deep breath.

"No, das enough," she interrupted. She patted Pili's cheek and then rested her hand there, cupping his jaw. "I done wit' all dis now. Let's jus' let it go."

"But Maile—"

"You make dinner tomorrow and take Albert fo' see da herd, and I like see my friends Monday."

"Yes, but, Maile, I want to—"

"Das it." Her voice was firm. When he looked at her, the lines on her face looked deeper, her eyes were puffy, and he didn't push to speak again. She was finished with the conversation. He would be, too.

He stepped toward the door to leave, and she called after him. "Be careful tomorrow, yeah. Albert, he's Dad's nurse."

Pili chuckled. "Don't worry, Mai. I'll make sure no cows trample him. I promise."

On Sunday Pili borrowed Harrison's truck to drive out to the winter pasture. From the ranch they took a wide two-lane road toward town. It curved through pasturelands—some theirs, and some belonging to other ranches—past the housing development they saw from the front porch and alongside a windbreak with trees hunched like a line of old women. In the afternoon light the fields were a deep gold. As they approached town, a cluster of children play-ing outside a red ranch house spotted the car and froze like statues. One boy couldn't stop giggling, though, and Albert laughed and waved at all of them. After the car passed, the children broke their poses and began to run around, tagging each other.

The farther they were from the house, the more both Pili and Albert relaxed, and the conversation took on more intimate tones. They spoke again of their families, but also of their schooling and college years. Pili described his first boyfriend and those initial exhilarating forays into clubs in the Castro District. Albert talked about the men in his nursing program who, while straight, learned to be supportive of him. "It was an education for all of us," he said.

Albert grew more pensive when he described former patients. "I did hospice care for a gentleman in Honolulu who was dying of AIDS. I shouldn't have been hired for the job. I was just ten months out of school, but I was the only nurse willing to take the position. This was when I realized how important white lies are. Here's this guy, who's dying, and he asks me if everyone is afraid of him. I said, 'No, I fought for this job.' The pay was great, so he might have believed me. And if he didn't, at least he didn't have to face that fear—to know that he was a pariah."

"But he had to know how the word 'AIDS' affects people. It's no secret."

"Yeah, but in some ways it doesn't matter if it's AIDS or cancer or any other disease. Dying is what makes someone a pariah. For some people, all they have at the end is their nurse. No one else will face death with them."

Pili wondered if he would have the strength to face death with his father. Maile certainly would. He hoped he would be like her at the end.

When they reached the access road to the winter pasture, Pili unlocked the cattle gate and drove the truck through. He had expected the herd to be in the ravine, hidden from view, but they were up by the road, their usual spot abandoned for reasons known only to them. "Will I scare them?" Albert asked.

"They won't know either of us. If my dad or Joe or Keo

were here, the cows would come to say hello. Especially to Keo 'cause he brings them mango skins and pineapple scraps."

"They eat that?"

"Sure, it's sweet. Keo spoils them."

"Will they stampede me?"

"You say something like that and I begin to wonder if you're really from this island."

"I grew up in Kona. I'm a city slicker."

Pili laughed. "Just keep away from the high-headed ones."

"High-headed?"

"The cows that lift their head when we step out of the truck. They're skittish. They can't be trusted."

Pili grabbed a blanket from the back of the cab and a plastic bag filled with pineapple cuttings and apples Maile had collected for them, a sign of her forgiveness. Albert followed Pili in an exaggerated tiptoe. "You can walk normally," Pili told him.

"Won't they hear me coming?"

Pili began to laugh again, but Albert was serious. "They'll hear you," Pili said. "They'll smell you. They'll see you. They know more about you than you know about you, but if you approach slow and cautious, they won't scatter."

The cows watched them. The animals lying in the grass turned their heads in the men's direction, and the ones standing shifted their bodies. Only one kicked back her chin so Pili could see the thick brown hair of her neck, and then she ran to the back of the herd. The rest were calm, but they kept their eyes focused on Pili and Albert, and when the men moved, the cows' eyes moved with them. "It's like *Children of the Corn,*" Albert mumbled.

They reached the first few cows, one of which lowed, and one of which took a step in the direction of the ravine. Albert paused and looked at Pili as if to ask if anything was wrong, but Pili smiled and held out a handful of pineapple scraps. A Charolais stepped toward him and wiped her long tongue along his hand and wrist. "Take some," Pili said, opening wide the bag of fruit scraps.

Albert took a few pieces and held out his hand with hesitation. A heifer moseyed over to him and licked up a piece of pineapple. "Their tongues scratch!"

The rest of the herd surrounded them then, the animals all wanting a taste of the fruit. Pili could feel the heat of their bodies and the rhythmic expansion of their sides as they breathed. Beside him, one of the animals quivered, her hide rippling like the surface of water in a breeze. Another swatted at a fly with her tail. Everywhere he heard the cows jostling for space, the soft, crunching sound of their hooves in the grass, and beneath him the sweet scent of their droppings rising in waves. Pili held out another bunch of scraps. An entire apple disappeared from Albert's hand. One cow tried to wedge herself into the center of the crowd, her head like the tip of a piece of pie and her backside sticking out, wide and round.

"Will she come after me?" Albert backed away, pressing his body against Pili's.

"We're out of fruit, so they'll lose interest in a minute." Pili scratched the ridge of a cow's back. Her belly was hanging low and her udders were engorged, so he knew she would be birthing within the month. She was early. The rest of the herd wouldn't begin to birth for at least another forty-five days.

Pili tucked the empty plastic bag in his back jeans pocket. The herd moved away slowly, the nervous ones first and then the others. Pili felt a soft tap on his buttocks, and when he looked, one of the yearlings was trying to get hold of the plastic bag with all the sweet juice on it. She scooted when he spun around, stopping ten feet away to observe him with Albert. Pili laughed, looking from her to Albert, and then Albert laughed, too.

Pili led Albert to the ravine. Behind them, the cows lowed, one to the other, or perhaps called for more sweets. He followed the edge of the ravine as it widened and deepened into a tiny canyon. The sun had passed behind the volcano, and the grass no longer resembled bronze but was a deep red river coursing down the incline of the field.

Amid the tall needle grass, Pili spread the saddle blanket so they'd have a place to sit, the blue one with the turquoise waves. Just the sight of it made him feel weightless, and he smiled again.

"Why are you smiling?" Albert asked.

Pili didn't know how to answer Albert's question, how

to explain the blanket's significance. "It's one of my dad's favorites," he started, then paused.

"It's beautiful."

Pili wanted to add that it had been his mother's engagement gift, a sign from Harrison to Mahea that he was ready to interweave his life with hers, but he couldn't think of a way to introduce the story. After several seconds passed in silence, Albert sat unceremoniously on the blanket and motioned for Pili to join him.

Pili laid back and spread his arms. They hung over the edges, in the high grass, and he could feel its sharp tips poking into his skin. When he rested his hands upon his face, thin scratches wound like bracelets around his wrists and forearms, and spots of blood gathered at the end of each cut.

He turned on his side to face Albert and noticed for the first time the sprinkling of silver in Albert's hair and the way his nascent beard curved over his cheeks and chin just as the grass curved over the topography of the land. A gust of wind blew through the ravine and Albert's hair stirred with the grass, and Pili laughed. He reached out a hand and let his fingers nestle in Albert's beard. Pili kept his hand there, longer than he intended, too long, until it seemed as awkward to draw away as to leave it against the side of Albert's face. Albert laughed nervously, perhaps feeling the same awkwardness as Pili did, or perhaps at Pili's unease, and then Albert took Pili's hand in his and lifted Pili's fingers to his lips. He wrapped his mouth around Pili's thumb, and his tongue was softer than Pili expected. Albert sucked gently. Without ever taking his eyes off him, he moved the thumb to Pili's forehead and rubbed a spot above Pili's left eyebrow. "You had some dirt there," Albert murmured.

The wind swept down Mauna Kea hard and fast now, and at first they were cold. But as the grass beneath the blanket yielded, they sank lower and lower to the ground, until they were shielded by the grasses and could no longer feel the wind. They pressed their faces next to each other, their mouths so close Pili could smell the fish Albert had eaten for lunch and see the delicate lines of red that flared through the whites of Albert's eyes. They kissed. Then they kissed again, more carefully this time, their tongues softly exploring each other's mouths.

Pili sat up suddenly—he wanted desperately to speak, to put into words his hesitations and fears, his hopes— but the wind stole his breath from him, and Albert lazily slung his arm around Pili's shoulders to pull him toward the ground again. Pili hesitated but then lowered himself and pressed his chest to Albert's and kissed him hard.

Albert's arms coiled around Pili's neck, and Pili's hands searched Albert's chest and shoulders, as if looking for handholds, for a way to better fit his body to Albert's. For a long time they pawed at one another like adolescents. The grass sliced into Pili's back and arms, but it didn't matter. He struggled against his shirt, the wind, even Albert, and the struggle felt exhilarating. But even as they writhed on the ground, hands caressing skin, mouths pressed together, Pili felt himself drawing away. Albert began to unbutton Pili's shirt, and Pili thought of Harrison clothed in those white sheets like a mummy.

He rolled onto his back, away from Albert. They were both breathing heavily—Pili watched Albert's chest rise and fall—but the wind took away the sound of their breath. "Are you okay?" Albert asked.

"He'll die soon, won't he?" Pili felt gripped by despair.

"Yes." Albert spoke without emotion.

Pili began to button his shirt. "Will he be in pain?"

"No. When the time comes, I'll administer more morphine. We'll make him as comfortable as we can. And then, eventually, he'll just stop breathing." Albert reached out his arms and drew Pili to him.

Pili pressed his face into Albert's neck. "I've never seen someone die," he admitted. Albert's skin was warm and soft and smelled sweet-sour like rice vinegar.

"It wouldn't matter if you had. It's different every time, and this is your father."

Pili wanted to ask Albert for a description of death—what it looked like, sounded like, smelled like—but he knew preparations were useless. If death was as individual as the life it took, then it would look, sound, and smell unique, too.

The sun dipped into the water and, with a final flash, slid from view completely. They stood and wiped the dust from their clothes and hair. Pili folded the blanket, and together they walked through the pasture toward the car. The cows watched them as they passed, and Albert waved as if the animals were old friends. Pili laughed and took Albert's hand. He felt light again, lighter than he had for weeks. On the drive home they listened to the radio play old paniolo favorites, the men's voices crooning softly in Hawaiian and the twang of their steel-string guitars filling the air.

"Joe and Keo bin hea yesterday. Dey stay talk story fo' long time, and I tol' dem I like fo' you help run the ranch." Harrison lifted the ledgers in his lap as if to hand them to Pili, but when Pili reached for them, Harrison set them upon his legs again.

Pili and Harrison were alone. Albert's shift didn't begin for another four hours, and Maile was in Kona to have brunch with a girlfriend. Pili felt proud of himself for having convinced her to go. He also felt giddy still from the evening before, from touching Albert and kissing him and the promise of what might follow. He had felt that same expectant nervousness while they ate dinner with Harrison and Maile, and he worried Maile might have sensed it. But she, too, was excited, happy to eat together as "one real 'ohana" and pleased to be cooked for, even if she did ask why Pili had purchased chicken when they had plenty of beef in the freezer.

"And what did they say?" asked Pili.

"Joe tink it akamai, da plan. He like if you check da money, da way it come and go. Keo, he no say much, but. He jus' like know you and da sista neva gon split da ranch. You know Keo, he wit' us folks since small kid time, and his papa, too, and he like see da ranch stay da kine. Same fo'eva."

"I would never let the ranch be split. Neither would Maile. Did you tell Joe and Keo I've got a job in San Francisco, and a life there, too? I won't be here to watch over things." Pili tried to sound firm, but part of him was wondering what might happen if he moved back to Waimea. Would Albert come out to his family in order to start a life with Pili?

"Ah, boy. You tink I no know dat?" Harrison looked down at his ledgers, and then up again. "But one day, in da future, you gon tink, 'Eh, I like fo' be dere, at home,' and den you gon come back. Until den, you help da sista. Approve da purchases, try make mo' sales, help wit' da marketing—dat what you do awready—and maybe you look into da kine organic beef dem uddeh ranches like do. You gon do evryting I do now."

"Dad, you do a lot more than that around here."

"Not so much anymoa."

"Maile's not going to like me taking over your role."

"You tink I care what she like?" he boomed. "Son, dis stay my ranch. I get fo' decide how it run. I no care what you or yoa sista tink. You go change it all when I ma-ke."

"Don't talk like that."

"What? When tell I go ma-ke, or when tell how you suppostu run da ranch."

"The ma-ke part."

Harrison snorted. "Mo bettah fo' me talk ma-ke dan tink you two no care fo' da ranch how I tell you fo' care." Harrison shifted in the bed, and this time he let Pili take the ledgers and place them on the other chair in the room. "Remember when you jus' one keiki? And da cousins come hea fo' da summer and you kids run everywhea. Ho, I tell you. I like give da whole lot dirty lickins, always in my way. But I neva trade it fo' nutting. All you, wit' auntie and da uncles and Joe and Keo. Dey still young den, too, and wild, dem."

"Those were good years."

"I like see dat fo' you and Maile."

"One day she'll remarry, Dad. She'll find a good man, and they'll have kids, and I'll come back in the summer to spoil those rascals."

"Ho, son, one day you gon have da kids and she gon spoil 'em. You bring yoa wahine hea, and da keiki, too, and teach 'em fo' ride. No, you let Maile teach 'em. Dat way dey stay on da horse." Harrison laughed so hard he began to cough.

Pili took a deep breath. He didn't want this line of thinking to go any further. "Dad . . ." Pili searched for the right words, the gentlest way to say what he needed to say. "I don't know if I'll be having kids. I don't know if I'll marry a woman."

"Son." Harrison reached his hand out and rested it on Pili's. "I know."

"You know?"

Harrison closed his hand around Pili's palm and squeezed. His father's skin was dry and soft as a summer wind, and Pili squeezed back. He felt exhausted with relief. "I know," Harrison repeated, nodding his head. "You still one young man. You still haf plenny wild in you. Settle down wit' one wahine? Ho! Tink neva can. But one day you gon change. I neva t'ought I marry and den I wen meet yoa mudda and bam. I neva move so fast! Awready forty, like one old man, me. And young, her. Beautiful."

"Dad," Pili said, trying to interrupt. The relief he had felt was turning into panic. He was desperate to make his father stop speaking.

Harrison ignored the intrusion on his monologue. "Find one like da momma. If can, love her. Treat 'er real nice. Do whateva you haftu fo' make her feel good, yeah? Das de ol' paniolo way. You lucky find one good woman, bettah keep 'er happy."

"Dad—"

"Ho, I tired now, Son. Like sleep." Harrison closed his eyes and folded his arms across his chest. "Can talk story afta dinna."

Pili sat in silence beside Harrison for a long time, wondering if he should wake his father, or if he should just let his dad live and die with a false promise of Pili's return, wife and kids in tow. Finally, he lowered the head of the bed with the hand crank to let Harrison sleep more easily and slipped from the room.

Albert arrived each evening as scheduled and took care of Harrison. After dinner, Pili joined them in the study. Harrison's energy was flagging now, but he grew animated when allowed to describe the types of grasses the herd ate and how the pastures were rotated and why he was angry about the fluctuating price of beef. Albert asked numerous questions, encouraging Harrison to remain engaged, and the conversation often wound to other topics, such as fishing for ulua or exploring lava tubes or the rumblings under Kīlauea that were all over the news. Eventually Harrison's eyes would droop or the pain would overwhelm him and he'd fall silent. Albert gave him the painkillers orally, but the time was close when even that would be impossible. Harrison had stopped eating.

As Harrison tried to find sleep, Pili and Albert sat in companionable silence. Sometimes Pili pretended to read and Albert actually read, and just to sit with their chairs side by side calmed Pili. In other moments, Pili wished he could take Albert's hand in his, or rest his palm on Albert's leg, or even smile at Albert in that private way a lover is allowed to, but Pili knew that in front of Harrison Albert would tolerate nothing but absolute professionalism.

After Harrison was asleep, however, Albert relaxed. He and Pili would leave the study to sit on the porch and stare out into the empty space of the night. Maile visited with them for a couple of minutes each evening, and, before she retreated to her bedroom, they spoke pleasantly about the weather warming and when the herd might switch pastures and which grains needed to be ordered for the finishing. While they waited for the light in Maile's bedroom to turn off, Pili and Albert whispered to each other, describing their boyhoods and memories with a sense of great urgency. Those nights felt coiled, like a towel twisted to squeeze out every last drop of water. Pili was determined to hear all of Albert's memories, every thought and emotion, every dream and lofty goal. He yearned to know everything about Albert, and for Albert to know everything about him.

When the house was at last dark, Albert checked on Harrison once more. Only then could Pili persuade him to walk down to the barn. Each night Pili showed Albert something new—Harrison's favorite saddles, the collection of spurs Keo kept in a gigantic wooden crate in one of the unused stalls, photographs of Joe's eldest daughter from the previous year's rodeo when she won in her age group for barrels. Eventually Albert would become nervous and push to return to the house. But the next evening, once Maile was asleep, Albert would let himself be lured to the barn again.

One night, Pili at last convinced Albert to climb up to the hayloft. At first Albert was unsure of himself. He was nervous that the old ladder wouldn't hold him. But when he reached the top, he breathed the air deeply and sighed. "I understand why you loved it up here as a boy," he said. Pili hung the electric lamp on a nail in one of the beams, and the yellow light trickled over them. Albert reclined against a pile of hay.

Pili rested his head on Albert's thigh, and Albert sank his fingers into Pili's hair to rub his scalp. "Being here, with you, makes me almost believe I could live on island again," Pili said.

"You are a man with a divided heart."

Pili kissed Albert's knee. He wondered if his longing to come out to his dad, yet his inability to do so, was also because of his divided heart.

Albert's fingers rifled through Pili's hair again, and Pili imagined Albert was sifting through his emotions like Maile sifted through rice when she was cooking. Pili let his body sink heavily against Albert's, and Albert's hands moved from Pili's scalp to his cheeks and then his lips. Pili unbuttoned Albert's shirt. They undressed each other without haste. Pili pressed his mouth to Albert's stomach and sucked softly at the small pouch of belly there. Albert's pubic hair smelled musty from sweat, and his hands had the blue antiseptic scent of the soap he used after working with Harrison, but despite these smells—or because of them—Pili desired him even more. Finally Albert pushed Pili facedown in the hay and climbed on top of him. He bit Pili's shoulder, then wound his tongue along the back of Pili's neck. Albert spread his arms over Pili's, interlacing their fingers. Pili stared at the light brown hairs on Albert's knuckles, and the dust clinging to the back of Albert's arms sparkled like the snow on Mauna Kea's peaks.

When they left the barn, Maile's bedroom light was on. Albert hastened his steps to the house. "Do you think she knows we were gone?" he asked, walking ahead.

"I'm sure Maile is just using the bathroom."

"I shouldn't have left your dad for so long." He took the porch steps two at a time.

"We weren't far. And we weren't gone for more than a half hour," Pili called after him, but Albert had already disappeared behind the screen door. Pili took his time walking up the porch steps. He was not going to indulge his fears. He was sure the light meant nothing. But even as he told himself to remain calm, he heard his sister running across the house to the kitchen phone.

"Nine-one-one?" Maile was crying. "I have an emergency."

Pili managed to sleep for a couple of hours, waking just after dawn with the scent of Albert's skin still on his body. He got out of bed hesitantly. Maile wasn't in her room, and the house was silent and tense. At the study Pili paused, afraid to go inside, afraid of what he might see. Would there be blood? Would Harrison look like himself? Would he be alive?

Albert sat in a chair beside the bed, his chin in his hand

and his eyes closed. He jolted awake when Pili stepped into the room and then, realizing it wasn't Maile, smiled sheepishly. Harrison looked like he was sleeping, and for a moment Pili forgot his father was in a coma. Harrison had lost consciousness the night before. "His body is shutting down," Albert had told Pili and Maile.

The EMTs had offered to take Harrison to the hospital—if he had had a stroke, which they suspected, then treatment might buy a small amount of time—but Maile had refused. "Nomo heroic measures," she said. "He neva want dat." The EMTs drove away with their lights off.

In the daylight Pili could see more clearly the changes in his father's body. The corner of his left eye drooped slightly, and his left arm and leg were immobile in a way that went beyond stillness and veered toward lifeless. The EMT had left an oxygen mask to replace the small tubes for Harrison's nose. The mask covered half his face.

"Talk to him," Albert said. "He can hear you. He won't be able to respond, but he can hear you."

Pili didn't know what to say. He wanted to both speak openly to Albert and use the right words with his father. He felt stretched in two directions. He would have liked time to think, but Albert was looking at him expectantly, and finally Pili said, "It's me, Dad. Pilipo."

"That's a fine start."

"I don't know what to say."

"Just keep talking to him. Let him know you're here."

"Can he understand me?"

"Scans show there's activity in the brain even when someone is unconscious like this."

Pili took a deep breath. "Dad, one of the EMTs was George Kapana's son. He remembered you. He said he still had the feather lei you made him all those years ago. Nice kid, yeah? He's getting married in a few months." Pili stopped. He felt strange delivering this kind of news to his father. After all, why would Harrison care if George Kapana's son was getting married? If he could hear Pili and think through what he was saying, then wouldn't he want to hear about his own family? About his present state? Pili felt immobilized. He wanted to say things that mattered.

He rested a hand on Albert's knee looking for comfort there, but Albert shifted in his chair. "Studies show that interactions such as these with family and close friends can actually prolong a patient's life."

Pili folded his hands into his lap. He felt alone. He thought of those boyhood evenings with his father on their porch when words were unnecessary. Pili stared at his father. The sheets were neatly tucked beneath the mattress and the blue and turquoise saddle blanket was folded over the bar at the foot of the bed. Pili ran his fingers along the blanket's edge where the fabric was beginning to fray.

In the kitchen a cupboard door slammed. "Did Maile sleep last night?" Pili asked.

"She's been cleaning since the paramedics left."

"She's pissed." Pili rearranged the saddle blanket so it covered Harrison's knees and feet.

"Can you blame her?"

"Nothing would have changed if we'd been here, right?"

"I doubt it." Albert paused. "It's possible, I guess." He refused to look at Pili, and finally Pili rose and left the room.

In the kitchen, Tupperware lids were strewn across the table. They looked like oversized jewels, red and blue and green, glowing in the kitchen lights. The mop and bucket leaned against the wall, and the room smelled faintly of bleach. Maile was on her knees, crouched behind one of the cupboard doors. "What are you doing?" Pili asked.

"Choke lids but I neva find one fo' fit my Tupperware." She threw a handful of lids into the sink and went back to pulling plastic containers from the cupboard. She moved quickly, constantly, like a waterwheel. Pili wanted to wrap his arms around her and force her to be still.

"How about I help you with this?" He gathered the lids in the sink and laid them with the others on the table. "Dad could use some new company," Pili said, smiling.

"He awake?" For a moment her movement ceased and she looked up at him with hope, but when he shook his head, she returned to the cupboard.

"Albert said we should talk to him."

"Albert like tell a lot of tings."

"Maile, don't be mad at him. I was the one who insisted on going to the barn. I was showing him Dad's blankets and the photographs of Joe's daughter and everything else."

She pretended to ignore him, but Pili saw her jaw throbbing beneath her cheek and knew she wouldn't stay silent for long.

"Albert feels terrible. The one night he agrees to go down there with me, and this happens."

"You like try tell me was one night, Pili?" Maile clambered to her feet to face him. Her hands were clenched around two lids that reminded him of green cymbals, and for a moment he wondered if she would try to clang them around his ears. "You tink I stay blind? You tink I neva see you and Albert go da barn evry night. And evry night, you gon long time. So I go sit wit' Dad. I wake up, and I go sit wit' him, and where you?"

Pili was bound in place.

"Tell me, Pili. Where you? You tink I no know?"

Pili tried to speak but faltered. All this time he thought he had hidden himself from her, and she had known. She knew about him. He was terrified, ecstatic, relieved.

"He woke up last night, you know. Dad woke up, and he wen aks where Albert stay and why I dere, and I tell 'im you and Albert go talk story, and he wen frown. 'Why dey no talk story hea?' ' 'Cause,' I tell 'im, 'Dey no like keep you awake. Jus' on da porch, dem.' See, I cover fo' you. But Dad know I no tell da trut'. He say, 'You look tired, sweetheart. Why you always do tings fo' Pili?' Das what he tell me, and den he wen close his eyes. So I fall asleep and when I wake up his breathing not right, and I tink, Why he look so heavy? And dat was it. He was gone in da coma." Her voice petered out along with her anger. Her shoulders slumped. Her bare arms, usually defined and muscular, seem to atrophy in front of Pili. He walked to her and pulled her to him. He wished to lift her into his arms and cradle her. She began to cry.

"I cover fo' you fo' years, you know."

"Covered for me? What do you mean?" He could feel her tremble against him.

"When Dad aks why you neva bring home one wahine, I tell him you work so hard no have time fo' date. Or I say you jus' broke up wit' one. Hard fo' find da right one. Das what I tell 'im."

Pili pushed Maile away from his shoulder and gazed down at her. "You told Dad those things?"

"What? You tink I like lie to him? Suppostu say what?"

"Say nothing." He released his grip on her and stepped backward.

"No, Pili. I haftu say someting. I haftu protect you, and him."

Pili felt his face grow hot with anger. "Protect us from what?"

"Each uddeh." She held open her hands as if a better answer rested there, and then she closed them into fists. "From hurt each uddeh. Das why you neva wen tell 'im, yeah? Or me. Das why you neva tell me? Neva like hurt me?"

"No. That's not why. I was just scared. I was protecting myself. Until this visit, when I began to think it was better if I came out to Dad. Then I wouldn't be scared anymore."

"Good you neva tell Dad. Fo' once you tink of us and not yoaself first."

"I never think of myself first," Pili protested weakly.

"Bulai you," she snapped. "Who flew to California? Who wen college? And who wen come hea in time fo' meet Albert?"

"I didn't know I was going to meet Albert here."

"You don' know what it's like fo' me." She bent over the sink as if an explanation lay in the pile of plastic lids. "All dis time, I take his jokes and his criticism and I neva complain because if I do den maybe he go turn on you and he question you and den it all gon fall apart."

"What would fall apart?"

"Us. Da tree of us. You, me, dad."

"You think I would make us fall apart? If I were myself, if I were out, we would all collapse?"

Maile stuck her chin out at him, defiant.

"How dare you. All these years you've thought if I came out, was open with him, it would be the end of everything. But you know what? I think you're wrong. I think Dad would have accepted it and we would have been better, stronger. Him and me. Maybe not you, but I don't care. If I could come out to Dad right now, I would."

Maile threw a lid across the room and it sailed like a Frisbee, landing on the floor beside the kitchen table. "Yeas ago, one ting. But now? What, you tink he want accept dis now? Good ting you no can tell 'im."

Pili slammed his fist on the countertop. "Can. Right now." He marched from the room. In the study, he lifted the turquoise blanket from the foot of the bed and held it in front of his father, as if Harrison could see it. Albert stood up from his chair, confused, and when Maile appeared in the doorway, he looked from Pili to her and back.

"Dad," Pili said. "You know how much this blanket means to me. Mom's blanket, the blue one. And I remember what it once meant to you and her."

Pili paused. He sensed his anger with Maile was driving him to act, and he wondered if he should give greater thought to the moment, but he suppressed these doubts. "I'd like to give this blanket to Albert. I want him to have it. I am giving it to him." Pili rested the blanket in Albert's arms.

"Why you gon do dis?" Maile whispered.

"Thank you," Albert said to Pili. He sounded surprised but pleased. After a moment he took Harrison's hands between his and pressed gently. "Thank you," he repeated, speaking this time to Harrison.

Maile remained in the doorway. "How can you?" She

looked stricken, more shocked than angry. "Not even yoas fo' give away."

Albert looked at her, confused and scolding at once. He clung to the blanket proudly. "Your dad means so much to me," he told her, and she shook her head. She looked ashamed or embarrassed or both, and Pili wondered if she felt guilty, or if the embarrassment was for him and Albert alone.

Pili no longer cared. He walked to the right side of the bed and rested his head on the pillow beside Harrison's. "I love you, Dad. You were a good father and a good man. And you have taught me to appreciate the goodness in other men." Pili didn't move then for some time, but remained with his head beside his father's. Albert continued grasping Harrison's hand, the blanket tucked beneath his arm.

Pili listened to his father's labored breath. He smelled his father's skin, redolent of Old Spice and age and death. He hadn't felt this much love for his father since he was a boy. He looked across the bed at Albert and smiled.

At last Albert smiled back. "I'm so proud to have helped your dad these last few months. This blanket is such a gift." Albert reached across the bed with his free hand and rested his hand on Pili's wrist. "You've been a good son." He spoke as if giving a benediction. Pili saw Maile turn and leave the doorway, but Albert never noticed.

The plastic lids were still strewn across the kitchen table when Harrison died. Eventually Pili put them away, not in any particular order, though he did try to keep the small lids stacked together because they were so easy to misplace. Maile wasn't speaking to Pili or Albert except to give them orders: call Auntie Inez, visit the mortuary, confirm with the florist. If Albert had thought his employment would end as soon as Harrison passed away, he had been mistaken.

Pili tried several times to apologize to Maile, but she only answered with more demands. "Need call Uncle Kawai in California," she said when he asked if she had wanted to keep the saddle blanket for herself, or "Dad like hea some Hawaiian songs, so bettah choose 'em," when he attempted to tell her he hadn't meant to be so angry.

Pili didn't feel remorse for coming out, but he knew his argument with Maile had driven him to it, and for that he was sorry. Her protection of him had hurt. In the end, both Maile and Albert were right. His coming out had less to do with his father than he had expected.

On the day of the funeral, family members flew in from Honolulu or drove over from Hilo or up from Kona. Joe and Keo were both pallbearers. Joe's middle daughter sang "Ku'u Home O Kahalu'u," and her clear, youthful voice lilted over her dad's guitar picking.

Keo hosted the reception—for once Maile could not bear to put the house in order—and the party lasted well into the night. Everyone wanted to meet Albert, who was a kind of hero, and many of the older women wrapped their arms around his neck and cried softly on his shoulder. He held them. He wasn't shy with the family or embarrassed, and he let himself be kissed and questioned and patted on the cheek.

At one point Maile turned to Pili and smirked, "Well, I guess he gon be a hit if you decide fo' marry." They were the first personal words she had spoken to him in six days, and they felt oddly good.

Sometime around midnight Albert said he had to drive home, but Pili could tell he had had too much to drink. Maile was asking to return home too, exhausted from the day, so Pili urged both of them into her truck. Keo was reluctant to see the three of them leave, and when Pili pulled out of the dirt roundabout that served as a driveway, the elder paniolo walked alongside the car. Finally, he shook Pili's hand and told him to drive safe. When Pili looked in his rearview mirror, Keo was watching them. He looked small in the glow of the house lights, standing alone in the center of that dark road. His hands were shoved deep into his pockets and he was hunched into himself. Pili and Maile weren't the only ones who had lost a father today.

Albert was laid out in the back of the cab, his head resting against the window and his legs slung on the bench seat while Maile curled up on the front passenger side.

Albert fell asleep, but Maile stayed awake, staring at the car's ceiling. "Dis day wen jus' how he like it." Her voice echoed in the cold cab. After a moment, she said, "I happy it's ova now."

"The funeral?"

She shook her head.

"Dad's dying?"

"Us, I mean. Da way we had fo' be. Das ova now."

Pili wanted to ask her what she meant by that, but she turned her face away from him and pressed her forehead against the window.

When they pulled into their driveway, all the lights were off, even the porch light, and the darkness emphasized the emptiness of the house. Maile said something about the horses needing to be fed, and as if on cue one of them whinnied, but neither she nor Pili made the move to head down to the barn. Pili knew the horses would have to wait to be hayed and watered until the morning. At least they had eaten well earlier in the day.

Inside, Pili pulled back the quilt on his bed and laid Albert down. Only three months ago this was Harrison's bed, before he'd become too weak to move and the hospital bed had been ordered.

Pili stepped into the hall. Maile was in the bathroom with the door closed. He flipped on the hall light: he was afraid to walk past the study when the lights were off. The hospital bed had already been removed, sent back to the hospice center from where they had rented it, and the two chairs that had once flanked the bed were now pressed into the corners of the room. The desk had yet to be moved back, and the room looked empty of life.

Maile stepped out of the bathroom, her face scrubbed clean except for the remnants of mascara that ringed her eyes and emphasized their redness. She came to stand beside Pili and stared into the dark study with him. He rested his hand on the small of her back and left it there, and eventually he realized she was crying quietly to herself. He drew her to him then, and her tears soaked through the thin cotton of his undershirt.

Pili was set to fly back to San Francisco in two days. He had invited Albert to join him, but Albert was hesitant and Pili suspected, despite their hopes for the future, that Albert would fail to depart the islands. Still, for some reason Pili couldn't articulate, he felt generous in the face of losing Albert. He hoped Maile and Albert would remain friends, or maybe he felt he owed Maile that friendship as some kind of apology. He wondered if, in time, Maile's allegiances would shift, and she'd tell Albert how Pili had betrayed him to Harrison.

Pili wanted to believe he would one day return to Big Island to stay. Perhaps by then Albert would be ready to come out to his family, and Maile would have remarried. Her kids would fill the barn with their laughter and their games and their thumping as they leaped from the hayloft rafters into the hay. Pili smiled to himself. His and Harrison's dreams for the ranch weren't different at all.

"Time fo' get some sleep," Maile said, pulling away from Pili. She patted his cheek, then took a step toward her bedroom.

He wanted to follow her, to sit beside her and lightly scratch her back. She had done this for him after their mother died. For weeks she remained with him until he fell asleep, even though he felt himself too old for such pampering. Years had passed since he had remembered her devotion during that period in their lives, but now he could suddenly feel her nails on his shoulder blades, the slow circles she drew as the heaviness of sleep overtook him.

"Have I helped you at all?" he asked. "At least sometimes?"

"Sometimes." Her face was puffy and flushed, and she looked older than she had a month ago. Still, she smiled at him. "Enough times." He wanted to ask if she had forgiven him or just stopped counting the myriad ways he had disappointed her. Maybe they were the same thing.

He wrapped his hand around her upper arm, gently, and felt there the muscle. She was strong, always had been. He imagined her strong arms holding a baby. He imagined her child in his own arms. He thought of the hayloft, of laying a blanket on the hay and showing her kids how to jump onto it from the rafters. He would describe foreign cities to them until their eyes shone with the possibility of travel, and then he'd tell them of the joys of returning home.

His hand dropped to hers and she squeezed it. "When you come back?" she asked.

"Soon," he promised. "As soon as I can."

ACKNOWLEDGMENTS

I am deeply thankful for my cohort at the University of Michigan and my fellow writers there, especially Sterling Schildt and the tireless Kodi Scheer, who has been as much an editor as a friend. I am grateful also to my mentors: Peter Ho Davies, Michael Byers, Eileen Pollack, and Nicholas Delbanco. The ideas for a couple of these stories first appeared in Joyce Carol Oates's class at Princeton University, and I owe a debt to her, April Alliston, and A.J. Verdelle for their encouragement.

The support I received from the Santa Fe Art Institute, Hedgebrook, Writers Omi at Ledig House, Ragdale, and the Kimmel Harding Nelson Center for the Arts allowed me to complete this book. My wonderful agent, Markus Hoffmann, lent his vision and insight to these stories. And at Hogarth, my editor, Lindsay Sagnette, along with Christine Kopprasch, buoyed me with the ideal combination of editorial precision and deep empathy.

My community in Hawai'i continually inspires and humbles me, and my interpretation of the islands is shaped in no small part by my friends and 'ohana on O'ahu and Maui. Tyler Noesen has left his indelible mark on each of these stories. Moreover, I would not be the writer or person I am without the friendship and support of Emily and the entire Essner clan. Mahalo nui loa.

I have been fortunate that I am descended, on both the Kahakauwila and Loy sides, from a long line of storytellers. These pages are shaped by my grandparents, uncles and aunties, cousins, and parents, as well as the histories they've shared with me, and I am in debt to my entire 'ohana, for by generously recounting their stories, they have taught me how to tell stories of my own.

ABOUT THE AUTHOR

KRISTIANA KAHAKAUWILA, a native Hawaiian, was raised in Southern California. She earned a master's in fine arts from the University of Michigan and a bachelor's degree in comparative literature from Princeton University. She has worked as a writer and editor for *Wine Spectator, Cigar Aficionado,* and *Highlights for Children* magazines, and taught English at Chaminade University of Honolulu in Hawai'i. At present, she is an assistant professor of creative writing at Western Washington University.